LA JOLLA SPINDRIFT

LA
JOLLA
SPINDRIFT

JACK TROLLEY

CARROLL & GRAF PUBLISHERS, INC.
NEW YORK

First Carroll & Graf edition 1998

Carroll & Graf Publishers, Inc.
19 West 21st Street, Suite 601
New York, NY 10010-6805

Library of Congress Cataloging-in-Publication data is available
ISBN: 0-7867-0513-2

Manufactured in the United States of America

For Willy Brueckel
A wondrous man.

Deep appreciation for the love and support of Tully MacIntire, Sarah Johnson, Robyn Ardez and Lynn Stanley. And special thanks for the make-the-book-work help of Kent Carroll, Adam Dunn, and, always there, Albert Zuckerman.

LA JOLLA SPINDRIFT

chapter 1

Saturday night. Donahoo is having a few drinks at The Waterfront tavern in San Diego's Little Italy. Old Crow in a chilled glass, no ice. He's listening to the smart talk. "If there was anything to evolution, Bo, a worm would have hands by now, and every husband would be deaf."

In limps the most beautiful woman he has ever seen in his whole life. A smudged angel in Calvin Klein's. Talking a Vassar girl's sophisticated dirty. Donahoo knows right away there is something amiss. She has her immediate pick of any guy in the place. A couple lawyers, a computer whiz, an aerospace engineer. The town's most successful condo developer or a yachtsman with a drinking problem. Any one of them, they're all declaring eligible, even those who aren't, but the lady isn't interested, she's slumming in the high rent district. She limps straight for him, Donahoo, like she's had him on her radar for a while, and she says, "Buy me a drink, sailor?"

Donahoo sets a record for finding his wallet, and they get to talking. She says her name is Jumpy. He says he's Tommy. She says she paints yellow daisies on brown paper bags. He says he solves mysteries. She wonders if he'd like to drive her home to Rancho Santa Fe. He says that's a long way. She says her parents are in Minnesota watching the ice break up. He says it's not that long a way.

The house is a mansion. It's so big it's got wings. It looks like it could fly. They start taking off their clothes as soon as they get through the door. She says she likes to do it while jumping up and down on the bed. Donahoo wants clarification of "do it." She confirms that she does indeed mean jump screwing. He doesn't see a problem with that but there is. Right away they're doing a Goldilocks. Her bed is too soft. The maid's bed is too hard. So they transfer to the California king in the master suite.

They go at it. They're at the top of their form—the highest they can jump, coupled—when suddenly a megawatt spotlight stabs through the French doors, lighting them up like a Nativity scene. It's so bright it would give a group heart attack to a herd of deer.

Prescott Havershot III, the head of American Steel, bursts into the room and screams, "What in the flying fuck do you think you're doing?"

Havershot's wife, Mildred says, "Now, dear, I'm sure there's an explanation."

chapter 2

Later, driving home, Donahoo would have called fate the force that conspired to suddenly turn his Toronado off Interstate 5, starting it on the twisty bluff road that led to La Jolla and the shimmering blue-black-silver of the day's newly revealed sea. The hand of fate, that is what he would say if anyone asked him later, but the fact was that he was still in shock from his unusual romantic tryst. Well, perhaps not unusual. It was more in the form of being unprecedented. He had been kicked out of bed plenty of times. Just never by the parents.

What a mess, he thought. Jumpy had not been as forthcoming as prudence might demand. She hadn't mentioned that she was really Travata Havershot, Prescott Havershot III's only child, and, as such, heiress to the American Steel fortune. Donahoo was accused of being a fortune hunter.

He fretfully tried to find someone to blame other than himself—Oscar, his cat, who, in old age, had taken to farting, driving him out of his tiny studio to the doubtful shelter of The Waterfront? Or, what seemed more reasonable, Travata Havershot, for shamelessly lying about her true identity, and for wanting to jump up and down with it stuck in her? Yes. Skip Oscar. Nobody was going to buy the goddamn cat. Pin the whole fucking thing on Miss Pussy-in-the-Sky.

That made him feel better but not much. Rancho Santa Fe disturbed him, and not because it was Jonestown, USA, where the Bo-Peep Heavens-Gate castration sect went the mass suicide route so as to catch a ride on a spaceship drifting in the tail of the Hale-Bopp comet. He was frankly uncomfortable around the monied-horsey set at "The Ranch." The exclusive community—sprawling mansions and gingerbread stables set amid riding trails and orchards on low, rolling, white-fenced eucalyptus hills—was only half an hour away from San Diego, but, in his mind, it was light-years apart. He could take yuppies and yachties, but the whip-and-spur guys were something else. They were not, by any stretch, mere mortals.

The fact was, Rancho Santa Fe was full of major movers and shakers, and one of them, Prescott Havershot III, would soon be shaking his tree. Havershot had taken the Toronado's license number. He'd be calling in a bouncing baboon complaint to headquarters first thing Monday. And Donahoo would never live it down, it would cling to him forever like dandruff.

He wondered how he could have been so stupidly tempted. Havershot was right—Travata was far too young for him. Twenty-five, at best; half his age. There was no weaseling out of his responsibility—he was the adult, right?—but he could make certain that it never happened again. He wouldn't call her and maybe she wouldn't call him. She hadn't given any indication that she intended to do so. They had just plunged into a can't-get-the-clothes-off-fast-enough, one-night stand. She'd never gotten around to asking his last name. She didn't know he was a cop. The closest he'd come was when he said he solved mysteries. He'd kept the Colt Python hidden.

Old Man Havershot, of course, if he followed up on the license plate, would learn his identity soon enough. One telephone call was all it would take. And Walter Saperstein, in his political correctness, in his police chief righteousness, was going to lower the baboon boom.

Donahoo winced in anticipation. He'd been imagining the worst the whole drive home. Removal—this would be the third time—from the helm of the San Diego PD's elite Squad 5, also known as SCUMB, for Sickos, Crackpots, Underwear and Mad Bombers. Reassignment to the Vice squad, to scout public toilets. Reassignment to Fraud, to count toothpicks. Saperstein had that kind of mind. He knew no mercy.

But Donahoo was haunted most by the memory of his pitiful attempts to impress Travata. He solved mysteries—had he actually said that? Jesus and Mary. He hadn't had an honest mystery in a year. His caseload consisted of the unexplainable. A little kid is standing on the sidewalk and a guy drives by and shoots him. How do you explain that?

So Travata wasn't the only one who had lied. He hadn't told the truth either. A murder mystery, given the current carnage, wasn't much of an operative term anymore, and he wasn't solving as many cases as he used to. Not because killers were getting smarter, they were getting dumber. They were doing the dumbest goddamn things you ever saw.

Ah, mysteries, Donahoo mused. He longed for an honest one. They had become so rare that he found himself watching for them, grabbing at whatever came along. Was that what was happening here? Maybe that was the reason he was headed, in direct defiance of Saperstein's verbal and written orders, for La Jolla and the foot of Nautilus and the palatial seaside estate of one Mad Marvin Molino. It wasn't fate, and it wasn't the trauma. It was the abiding mystery that resided there. And the fact that the shit he was currently in couldn't get any deeper.

What he'd do, he thought, he'd just drift by, take a quick peek, see who was doing what. Mad Marvin was a mad killer. There was a federal warrant outstanding. They couldn't just let him go. Could they?

Donahoo wasn't sure anymore, that was the mystery. Why, in three months, had nothing, ab-so-lute-ly nothing, happened to Mad Marvin? *Nada.* Nobody would tell him anything, even though, in a sense, it was his case. He'd made the guy. Dumb luck, yes, but that didn't detract from it, because he was the one who'd agreed to partner with Cominsky, and it was Cominsky, newly into his Compost Period, who had wanted to use his Sears credit card to buy a Little Heap Composter.

It was predestined after that.

The only Sears was in La Jolla and it didn't have any Little Heaps. To make up for it, Cominsky had suggested the Veggie Special at Sammy's California Wood-Fired Pizza, and it was there that they were seated next to Mad Marvin. Cominsky didn't know the guy from shopping. "He owns a furniture store, right?" he'd ask later, but Donahoo knew Mad Marvin right away as the Chicago Mob's worst killer from the cover of an old *Time* magazine, which he'd previously come across in his dentist's office. It wasn't a face that was easily forgotten. It was strangely empty, the eyes almost blank, the look of a man for whom nothing mattered—yet it allegedly sheltered unspeakable rage. Positive ID. Mad Marvin Molino. Who, according to *Time,* was supposed to be hiding out, after significant plastic surgery, not only from the feds but also rival mobsters, in Rio de Janiero.

They had done it strictly by the book. No big scene at Sammy's. No provoking a gun battle with innocent people around. Instead, quietly, carefully, Donahoo and Cominsky had followed Mad Marvin's big black limo to his walled estate at Windansea Beach. Whereupon, by the book, they had reported Mad Marvin's presence in San Diego to Lewis, captain, Investigations.

Whereupon the case had fallen into a hole.

No adequate explanation had been put forward. Lewis simply shrugged and said it had gone to the FBI. Saperstein said it was with the Bureau of Alcohol, Tobacco & Firearms, and Cominsky was convinced it was with the CIA. "Remember Kennedy and The Mob?" Cominsky said, which didn't prove anything, but he thought it did.

That had been three months ago. Donahoo thought it was time to find out what was going on.

chapter 3

Molino's estate was one of a kind, the biggest and probably the best property on all of Windansea. Certainly it was the most private, separated from its neighbors by small bays with treacherous cliffs, and hidden from passersby by a twelve-foot brick wall that would never again be permitted by the Coastal Commission.

Donahoo slowly drifted by in the gray rain. Half a block of adobe, buildings and patios, a swimming pool, a spa, no lawn. The main house had a "great room," a library, a professional kitchen, six bedrooms, four baths, and three fireplaces. The guest house had two bedrooms, two baths, and a fireplace. There was also a four-car garage, on-site parking for a dozen more vehicles, and two stairways down to the beach.

Donahoo hadn't been inside. He knew it only from photographs in *Rich & Famous Properties,* where it had been featured at length the previous February, listed for $4.5 million. He also knew, from checking county records, that Mad Marvin, when he purchased it in June, had paid only $3.8 million. He had also negotiated down the commission. The Realtors had been happy with—well, who knows if they were happy?—they had split two percent.

A tough guy, Donahoo thought. Not the kind of person you'd want to argue with. He passed the estate and stayed on the beach road. He was looking for a stakeout but couldn't spot anybody. He thought that was strange because he didn't think they'd be that good. Donahoo's opinion, based on personal contact and experience, was that the FBI couldn't watch a movie. They thought they were too good for stakeouts. So they got too easily bored and pissy. They missed things. He drove as far as the Windansea Pump House. Then he turned around and drove back. The street was empty as far as he could see. No sign of anybody.

Well, if they weren't staked out in the street, they had to be in one of the neighboring houses, he decided. It would be expensive—three thousand a month, minimum—but maybe they'd found a place to rent? They had that kind of stick-the-taxpayers money. He hadn't thought of it earlier because there were so few vacancies for prime beach-front property. But in three months? Something could have opened up.

He slowed and almost stopped. He wasn't looking for a supposed surf bum's van with too much electronics junk anymore. He was looking for a movement at a dark window in the row of townhouses across the street. If there *was* a stakeout, it was inside somewhere, across the street, or up the hill a ways, on an angle providing an unobstructed view of the estate.

He suddenly felt vulnerable to unseen spying eyes. He picked up speed. He ought to leave, he thought. He hadn't learned anything, and he wasn't going to.

Up ahead, a little black Tercel appeared out of nowhere, angling across the street and parking illegally, facing in the wrong direction. A man got out and then a woman. They were neatly dressed and had identical briefcases. They looked determined. They walked directly up to Mad Marvin's wrought-iron gate and rang the bell.

Donahoo watched. Avon, he thought, but then immediately realized his mistake. It was Sunday morning. They were Jehovah's Witnesses.

They rang the bell several more times. There was no response. Finally, the man indicated to the woman that he wanted her to make a stirrup with her hands and boost him over the wall.

Oh, Jesus, no! Donahoo thought. He pushed out of the Toronado and hurried up the sidewalk, yelling, "Hey! Don't do that!"

Too late. The man, surprisingly agile, was atop the wall. He grinned triumphantly and dropped out of sight.

Donahoo ran up to the woman. "Do you know whose house this is?" he demanded.

She looked at him brightly. "Does it matter?"

"Usually," Donahoo told her. He ran to the gate. The man was angling across the driveway in the manner of someone rushing the house.

The front door burst open. Molino came out dressed in pajamas. His face was livid with rage. He was holding a large revolver. He moved into position with an odd, twisted gait.

"Who ya fucking with, fishbait?!" he screamed. He took careful aim and squeezed off three quick shots.

The man staggered and slumped to the driveway. Molino turned abruptly and went back into the house. The door slammed.

Donahoo gripped the wrought-iron gate. The man was very still.

"What happened?" the woman asked. She had a glazed expression—one of shock and disbelief.

Donahoo didn't answer. He was almost as shocked. He thought that maybe it was a terrible mistake. *Time* had mentioned that there was a contract out on Molino. Mob rivalry. Bad blood. It had been wrong about the plastic surgery and the hiding out in South America. But maybe it had been right about the contract. Maybe Molino was trigger-happy, he figured the Witness was a hit man, and maybe he was so enraged because his bodyguards were obviously sleeping on the job?

Donahoo took the woman by the arm and led her to the Toronado. He put her in the back seat and told her to stay there. She still couldn't accept what had happened. She nodded numbly.

He thought very briefly about going in the house and bringing out Molino. He was deterred by the "coulds." The guy *could* have six bodyguards in there. They *could* be awake by now. They *could* be armed with howitzers.

Donahoo drove to the pay phone by the Pump House. He called headquarters and reported what had happened. He delicately suggested it was a job for the SWATs.

The officer taking the call was elated. "You can nail Molino to the cross!" he yelled.

Yeah, maybe, Donahoo thought, then again maybe not. Molino was a powerful mobster with a lot of bad connections. Donahoo could see himself nailed up there.

chapter 4

"I don't know about you, Tommy," Saperstein said. "How could you not realize the girl was a little off?" He posed the question as he entered his office, in the act of removing a bone-dry trench coat that had proved unnecessary, since it hadn't rained as forecast. "She's got a lift in her shoe."

Donahoo, waiting with Lewis, captain, Investigations, and the other members of Squad 5, Cominsky, Palmer, and Gomez and Montrose (the fabled team of Spick and Spook) decided that was a semi-rhetorical inquiry. It did not require an answer at the moment. But it would eventually.

Saperstein, a tall, thin, scholarly model of efficiency, smiled his bookkeeper's smile and continued with his choreography. To the un-initiated, this might be mistaken for a prelude to the Dance of Love, but Donahoo recognized it as the Fox-trot of Death. The four-buckle trench coat went into the eighteenth-century Sheraton-style armoire. The suit jacket, a dark blue pinstripe, an Yves Saint-Laurent, was draped over the bow-back Windsor chair with wheel-shaped splat and H-shaped stretcher. Saperstein's close-cropped graying hair was smoothed into place. The shirtsleeves were unbuttoned and rolled up two exact turns. His dark horn-rimmed glasses were lowered a quarter inch on his longish nose. Notes, lengthy notes, were removed from the jacket, placed on the Louis XIV desk, next to the yellow legal pad and the three freshly sharpened pencils. Donahoo divined the notes as being from a telephone call from Prescott Havershot III.

"Wherever this goes . . ." Saperstein began. He finally sat down and stared disgustedly at Donahoo. The pad and pencils were pushed aside with the calculator and phone. He leaned forward, his suspenders straining, blood in his eye. His desk was no longer a desk. It was a killing floor. "Wherever this goes—and it could go almost anywhere—I'm holding you personally responsible."

Donahoo knew what Saperstein *should* hold. He should find a brain and hold it between his ears. He had the biggest case of the year in front of him, the arrest of Mad Marvin Molino on a first-degree murder charge. The *Union-Tribune* had a headline about it the size of "GERMANY SURRENDERS," and he was ignoring it in favor of the Travata Havershot misunderstanding.

"This girl was in a traffic accident, did you know that?" Saperstein continued, talking more to Lewis and the Squad 5 investigators than to Donahoo. "Her left leg was injured. Made shorter. And, of course, there was also the head injury . . ." Saperstein paused to look at Donahoo, ". . . which accounts for her peculiar taste in men."

Donahoo suddenly tuned in. "Huh?"

"That's correct," Saperstein said smugly. "Brain damage. Physically, mentally, the woman is twenty-six. But emotionally?" There was another pause. "Emotionally she is twelve. She doesn't discriminate. She will chat up anybody."

Donahoo was staring. "What?"

"You heard me. The pitiful creature . . . no fault of her own . . . is a relentless slut." Squad 5 turned en masse to look at Donahoo. They were his men, tested, loyal. Donahoo was certain they would follow him anywhere. But he wasn't sure they could let this opportunity pass. He was right.

Palmer, a cocky little crewcut ex-bantamweight who always had to prove how tough he was, said, "A no-brainer, huh?"

Montrose, who was smarter than all of them, who looked like a movie star and had even more to prove, said, "Twelve? Did you carry her books?"

Lewis hitched up his pants, even though he was sitting down. He said, accusingly, "You couldn't tell?"

"Uh," Donahoo stammered. He wondered if he was flushing; his neck felt hot. "I guess I knew something was wrong. But I, uh, you know, didn't put it down to brain damage."

"The lift should have been a clue," Saperstein complained.

"You can't blame the Sarge," Cominsky said, rising to Donahoo's defense. "There are lotsa women like that."

"With lifts or brain damage?"

"Both."

Saperstein gave Cominsky a withering look. For a moment it appeared he might ask him about his plastic Vons shopping bag, which contained the food scraps he'd been picking up all weekend, for his Little Heap Composter. The bag was bulging and smelled pretty ripe.

Donahoo tensed. Cominsky was Squad 5's geek. He was a string bean, gawky, uncoordinated. He got all his clothes from the thrifts and his tastes ran to the bizarre. He had once embraced a bee-yellow jacket. He was wearing a chartreuse one now. Saperstein was always looking for ways to get rid of him on account of his weird ideas. But Donahoo thought that Cominsky's weird ideas were exactly what made him so invaluable to the squad. He had ideas so weird that sometimes they were brilliant. Admittedly, though, his present passion, gathering compost items while on duty, didn't fall into that category.

"Is that you, Cominsky?" Saperstein asked, sniffing.

"No sir," Cominsky lied, or perhaps he was just unaware. He'd been blanking out a lot since becoming a vegetarian. He would drift off into space on the slightest pretext. On the positive side, though, he was no longer constipated, and was, in fact, daily enjoying what Gomez called the *poop du jour*.

Saperstein considered and then reclaimed the notes he had taken during the call from Havershot.

"You picked her up in a bar, Tommy?" Saperstein said, refusing to quit. "That surprises me. There are easier ways, you know. I see ads in the paper every day. 'Life explorer seeks intelligent, passionate, financially secure black male with large can opener who likes Cajun food. *Sprechen sie Duetsch?'* "

Donahoo didn't respond. There was no use saying anything. Saperstein had the ball and he was going to run with it. He was going for the whole hundred yards. Nobody could stop him.

"Jumping up and down on the guy's bed. With your dick in his daughter. His *demented* daughter."

Donahoo refused to dignify it with a reply. He made no response.

"It says here the *mother* saw you?"

No response.

"It says your clothes were scattered all over."

No response.

"It says you kept your socks on. Why is that?"

No response.

"Well, let me tell you something, Tommy," Saperstein said, putting the paper aside again. "Repeat. I'm holding you responsible. I don't want you going anywhere near this Travata Havershot. No more of this Lovers' Leap. From now on, you don't wanta jump in bed, you especially don't wanta jump *on* the bed. She is off-limits, period, end of story. It's all over. You haven't creamed off just any jackshit father here. This is Prescott Havershot III. He's got money and he's got power. He says piss, the streets turn yellow."

"Yeah. He told me."

"You romance his little girl again, he can have you destroyed."

"He told me that too."

"Okay," Saperstein said, finally letting go. "We'll leave it at that. Ordinarily, I'd cut your pecker off, but seeing how you got lucky with Mad Marvin, you're being granted a pardon." He went through the pile on his desk and found Donahoo's report on the Jehovah's Witness shooting. Finally, he was taking up Molino, who, in the course of 24 hours, had been arrested, booked, and charged with first degree murder. It was a major coup. Donahoo had been on the TV. "DA Davis says you're the whole case."

Lewis hitched his pants again. He had been called in from his vacation to direct the San Diego Police Department's coordination with the FBI. He still didn't know anything official about the incident;

this was his first briefing. "What about the victim's wife? Didn't she see the shooting too?"

"That's unclear. She says she did but her story differs from Donahoo's."

Lewis turned to Donahoo. "Did she see it?"

"I dunno," Donahoo admitted. "I was looking at Molino, not her. What I think, though, she was in the wrong position, the wall was in the way. She wouldn't have got to the gate until after the shots. Molino was back inside the house." Donahoo hesitated. He was still a little miffed at Saperstein for his Alcohol, Tobacco & Firearms bullshit. "What's the stakeout say?"

Lewis's interest revived. "Hey, that's right. The stakeout must have seen something."

"What smartass knows," Saperstein said, glaring at Donahoo. "This caught them at a bad time. Change of shift. One left before the other showed up."

Donahoo hoped he was looking all innocence. "Really? Who screwed up? Don't tell me it was the ATF?"

"Or the CIA?" Cominsky offered.

"Keep pushing," Saperstein told Donahoo. He turned back to Lewis. "This is moot. We've got Tommy. We don't need the wife." He shoved the report across his desk to Lewis. "DA Davis doesn't want to go with a Jehovah's Witness anyway. He says, you know, who's gonna put any credence in somebody who's been wrong four times about when the world's gonna end?"

Lewis picked up the report. He put on his glasses. He started reading and stopped abruptly. "No murder weapon?" he asked Saperstein.

"No. It was gone by the time we stormed the place. Like DA Davis says, Tommy is the case, it's a good thing he was right on top of it, they're gonna bring in six clones who'll say they were all there when it happened."

Saperstein sorted through his pile again. He found something that seemed more interesting.

Donahoo was thinking about Travata Havershot. He didn't buy it. Not completely. Yes, maybe she was off, but not completely off, he thought. The woman had her problems. But she knew *exactly* what she was doing. She had it down pat. And up.

"Okay," Saperstein said. "Next topic. Panhandlers at stop signs." Lately he had become a hands-on police chief interested in the smallest detail. Nothing was too unimportant for his personal attention. It had been variously attributed to a mid-life crisis or the shingles. "The mayor is chewing my ass. This is supposed to be America's Finest City and we've got all these bums standing around with messages scrawled on scraps of cardboard. 'NEED FOOD. GOD BLESS.' She says it spoils our image. I talked to Traffic. They agree they're a distraction. Motorists are going through stop signs because they don't want to stop next to these guys. It makes them feel guilty if they haven't got any loose change."

Palmer said, "Who cares?"

Gomez, the squad's fashion plate, a Beau Brummell Mexican who had been sucking up lately, said, "The people they hit when they go through the stop signs."

Saperstein, smiling benevolently, said, "Exactly. We've had a broken leg and a couple cracked ribs and a severe case of amnesia. We need to do something before there is a fatality. Now here's my idea . . ."

Lewis was still reading the Molino report. "I take it we're finished with Mad Marvin?" he asked.

Saperstein frowned. "What else is there?"

"Well," Lewis said uncomfortably, "It says here . . ." He stopped and glanced at Donahoo. "It says Mad Marvin just laughed when he was arrested. He bragged he'd never go to trial because Donahoo wouldn't live to testify."

Donahoo didn't remember reading that. He took the report from Lewis. He saw that it had been revised to include statements from one of the SWATs who took Molino into custody at Windansea.

"It sounds like a threat to me," Lewis said.

"Oh?" Saperstein's expression suggested that had never occurred to him. "So what are you saying, Lewis? You want to throw in a threatening charge? Molino gets two months added to his death sentence?"

Donahoo was reading Molino's threat. There was a direct quote. "That spud who says he saw me pop the 'hovah? I swear he's gonna lose his eyes. He'll never take the stand," it read.

"What do you think, Tommy?" Lewis asked.

"I think it's a racist slur," Donahoo told him. He handed the report back. "Will you listen to this spaghetti? He's calling me a potato?"

"That's not a threat," Saperstein said. "You want to worry about somebody, Tommy? Worry about the FBI. The reason they didn't move in right away on Mad Marvin? They were watching him in a case involving something bigger than murder. You fucked it up. Their case is in the toilet. They gotta start all over."

"I knew it," Cominsky said. "CIA."

"How come you never told me?" Donahoo wanted to know.

Saperstein pretended not to have heard. "Now here's my idea. Montrose pretends that he's a bum."

"Me?" Montrose said indignantly. His face shimmered with anger and dismay. "Because I'm black? Right?"

"No," Saperstein assured him. "Not at all. It's because some of these bums have been hit by cars on account of they're standing too close to the stop signs. And with your natural athletic ability it's easier for you to jump out of the way."

Montrose appealed to Donahoo. "Sarge, do something here, will you? It's because I'm black."

There was a popping noise and a strange smell drifted out of Cominsky's compost bag. It was an odd combination not readily identifiable. Donahoo thought it might be broccoli, rancid chicken, and horse manure. It also might be Zyklon B.

"Is that you, Cominsky?" Saperstein asked.

Cominsky didn't answer.

Saperstein said, "Speak up!"

Donahoo, sensing the worst, said a silent prayer. Saperstein was out for somebody's scalp this morning. If he couldn't get Donahoo on account of his being a star witness to the Witness whack, he might settle for Cominsky. "You know, you're getting awfully slow, Cominsky," Saperstein said. "I don't think we need slow cops. I like to think we need fast cops. Have you got a read on that?"

Cominsky was thinking. Donahoo was thinking too. But he couldn't think of anything to say in Cominsky's defense.

"Well, uh," Cominsky said slowly. "Not necessarily." He took the compost bag off his lap and put it under his chair. "We've been talking about motorists here? What I've noticed, old people drive slow, and everybody thinks it's because they're old, but what if it's only slow people who grow old? What if fast people don't grow old? What if that's why you don't see old people driving fast? So maybe, this is just a suggestion, you may want to rethink your fast theory, Chief."

Donahoo looked in awe at Cominsky.

"I've been thinking about it," Cominsky explained. "It goes with being a vegetarian and a composter. These things complement each other. They all come together to form a Life Wisdom. Sometimes I think I'm gonna live forever. I'm never gonna die, Sarge. Somebody's gonna have to kill me."

Saperstein stared for a long time. "The word is *slowly*," he said, "Slow-ly. Let me hear me you say it. Slow-ly."

Cominsky carefully obliged him. "Slow-ly."

"By God, I think he's got it," Saperstein said. He turned to Montrose. "Now. About this black business. Let's see if there is something we can do about it. Have you ever considered painting yourself? You could do it gradually. Start with an off-white."

Montrose looked to Donahoo for help. Donahoo shook his head. He hadn't helped Cominsky and he couldn't help Montrose. He couldn't think of anything but his own problems. He was wondering about Prescott Havershot III and Mad Marvin Molino. Both had threatened to put his lights out. He wondered if they were serious and, if so, how serious. He wondered what he could do about it. Probably not much. He was thinking about the FBI. It was pissed at him too. He was thinking about Saperstein. For a hands-on police chief, the guy was all thumbs, he thought.

chapter 5

Donahoo walked out of the San Diego Police Department in a manner befitting Saperstein. He thought of himself as going into the new day's unexpected warm sunshine, and simultaneously into the cold dark shadow of death. He could feel it, taste it. It was wet on his palms and bitter in his mouth. *This soon?* he thought, caught up in his own melodrama. He hadn't figured they would come after him so quickly. He thought that his life's sport was suddenly over. He wasn't the hunter anymore. He was the quarry.

He walked out into the middle of Broadway. He stopped there and made a slow, full circle. Looking at all of the places, the rooftops and balconies, the windows and doorways and dark crannies where a sniper with a high-powered rifle might be squeezing the trigger. The guy could be hiding anywhere.

The Alcazar apartments. That would be a good place. On a rise—clear, unobstructed line of fire. Next to an I-5 on-ramp—fifteen minutes away from Tijuana. Easy shot, easy getaway. Donahoo turned again. Yeah, anywhere, he thought. El Campo Ruse. Sudden Impact Paintball Arena. San Diego Bindery. The Salvation Army Adult Rehabilitation Center. Rescue Autos Towing. Maybe the eyes in the pineapple person painted on the wall of the charity food depot were actually peepholes? He was getting paranoid. He wondered how the hell he was supposed to protect himself.

A car was coming. The driver was looking at him apprehensively. He waved it past and then returned to the sidewalk. Well, he'd just have to do something, he thought. He couldn't wait. He couldn't be passive; it wasn't his nature.

"What's the matter, Tommy?" Lewis called across the parking lot from his department Crown Victoria. He was on his way to talk with the FBI. "You're looking a little down in the shorts."

Yeah, Donahoo thought. He was. But he hadn't thought it was so obvious at a distance. He tried to smile, but it didn't work.

"You need to talk to somebody?"

Yeah, Donahoo thought again. But not you. Lewis was a worn old crab who had spent the last ten years talking up his retirement, and now they couldn't run him out with stink bombs. He had changed his mind after a couple of months at home with only his wife to amuse him. He was back as a "Consultant," and holding down, through Saperstein's sleight-of-hand, his old job as captain, Investigations. Donahoo couldn't recall getting any fatherly advice from Lewis that turned out to be particularly helpful. It ran to the well-why-don'tcha-jump-off-a-bridge kind of advice.

"Talk to me."

"Naw." Donahoo had lately considered a return to Catholicism. This might be a good time to pursue it. He'd had a few meetings with Father O'Malley at St. Jude's. He'd mentioned it to Lewis. "I think I'll talk to a priest."

"O'Malley?" Lewis shouted. "That Franciscan faggot flute? He's been on his knees so long he thinks he's four-foot-eight. He doesn't know if he's praying or advertising a blow job." He was driving away. "Don't talk to me about O'Malley!"

Donahoo watched him go. He thought that society asked too much of police officers. It asked them to be patient, fair, restrained. It asked them to be honest and to resist temptation. It gave them the power of life and death and asked them to deal with the scum of the earth. It asked them to sleep well because tomorrow was another day. He thought that the burden was sometimes overwhelming and that Lewis, who didn't know when to quit, who couldn't, was a good example of what happened to a guy, given those pressures. Donahoo also thought that maybe he'd pass on O'Malley.

Lewis made the turn out of the parking lot. He was going so fast the oil pan hit the exit ramp. There was a shriek of tortured metal. The Crown Victoria bounced, squealed a block-length of Fourteenth, and turned west on Broadway, headed downtown.

Donahoo got in Squad 5's vehicle of choice, a battered, rusted-out, burgundy/gold Dodge SE 250 Ram van. It could be used, if required, for surveillance. It embodied the adjective "nondescript." Cominsky was waiting in the passenger side captain's chair. His compost bag was at his feet. He was reading a brochure titled "How to Eat Your Way to a Better Sex Life."

Cominsky said, "What was that all about?"

"The oil pan hit," Donahoo said.

Cominsky, looking at him now, said, "I mean O'Malley."

Donahoo told him, "I think they're the same thing, and if you keep drinking that wheat grass, we're gonna have to mow you."

"He loves you, you know that?" Cominsky said, putting the pamphlet aside. He added, in reference, apparently, to something he had read, "The secret is kale."

Yeah, Donahoo thought. He knew all about love. He'd been loved before. He got on Broadway, heading east, the opposite direction of Lewis, toward Golden Hill. Death might lurk but Duty called. He had to see a snitch, Clancy Holden, and he had to track an ex-Navy SEAL, Willie Johnson, whom he suspected of sinking a sloop in San Diego Harbor.

The reason he suspected Willie was that the Coast Guard thought it was the work of someone trained in underwater demolition. So he had checked with the Navy and learned that Willie was the only San Diego-based SEAL to have been discharged in the past two years. He'd gone out a few months ago on a dishonorable. No details yet. Still, suspicious. Also, Willie was from Golden Hill. That in itself might not be suspicious but it was guilt by association.

"It's about Mad Marvin," Cominsky said. "Lewis thinks the guy is totally berserk. He's afraid the guy is gonna whack you."

"Mad Marvin?" Donahoo was watching the road. There was a bum standing in the middle of it. "Oh, yeah? Mad Marvin's in jail."

"His friends aren't."

"Yeah. And they wanta stay out. They wouldn't come after me."

"Why not?"

"Because it's an unwritten law. Never pop a cop."

"Why not?"

"Because the full might of an aroused justice system would descend upon them. They would be relentlessly pursued. There would be no escape. They would be found and destroyed."

"Are you okay?"

"No."

What Donahoo knew about Molino, he'd read in *Time,* most of it. He still wasn't privy to the FBI file. Lewis was supposed to get it. *Time*'s version was almost surreal. A Mob killer who reputedly makes big hits for big money. He waits for the phone to ring, then disappears. When he resurfaces, somebody important is dead or missing. Mostly they were missing. Does that kind of guy have friends? He can pay almost four million cash for a house. He's probably got a lot of friends, Donahoo thought glumly.

"Well, I only know what I see in the movies," Cominsky said, which was probably true. "They're laying it on, sure, everybody says 'fuck' five hundred times in every scene, but if there's any truth at all to the depictions, you could be in real trouble, Sarge. They're super pricks and they form sacred alliances. They'd kill Clint Eastwood if there was a dime in it. I don't think being a cop is any protection at all in this situation. You heard what Saperstein said. You're the case. Mad Marvin takes a walk if you can't talk."

"What is this? You trying to make me feel good?"

"I'm trying to tell you why Lewis is upset."

Donahoo didn't answer. He too wished he knew more about The Mob. Mad Marvin was the first Mafioso of any real consequence to ever show up in San Diego. There wasn't the kind of action here that would attract them. They worked Vegas or LA. They rested in La Costa and Palm Springs. They passed on San Diego. Still, Saperstein always had somebody looking for them. He wasn't satisfied just to have the Mexican Mafia and the Asian gangs and the Bloods and the Crips and a tidal wave of scum from Tijuana. He wanted it all. But no major Mafiosa had shown up, until Mad Marvin.

"What would you propose I do?"

Cominsky looked baffled. He hadn't expected the question. Finally he said, "Live life to its fullest?"

Donahoo sighed. He was like Cominsky. He didn't know fuck-all about The Mob. What he had he had gotten from reading newspapers and watching movies. Now his life was on the line and his reference point was Al Pacino.

chapter 6

Clancy Holden was finishing up a wash at the Coin Laundry at Twenty-fifth and Broadway, in a little mall next to Humberto's 24-Hours Tacos and a Finest Donuts. Donahoo parked and went over to see her alone. He couldn't trust Cominsky in Clancy's presence. The guy was apt to say anything, like promise her immunity or something. Cominsky couldn't help himself—he was in love. It was best to leave him in the van.

"Tell her hello!" Cominsky cried to Donahoo's back.

Donahoo waved off the request and pushed inside the laundromat. Clancy looked up from folding white lace panties. He'd thought she had a kind of dumb name until he met her cousin, South America. She looked past him and into the parking lot, where, Donahoo knew without looking, Cominsky was hanging out of the van, grinning stupidly.

Clancy said, "What's with him, anyway?"

"I think it's kale," Donahoo said.

The fact was though, he had to admit it, Donahoo found Clancy just as fascinating as Cominsky did. She wore her hair in two pigtails that stuck out like handles from each side of her head. Until Travata came along, Donahoo had always considered Clancy to be Best of Show. She was a mix—black, Indian, Chinese. She had it all together. Full lips and almond eyes. Cheekbones like burial mounds. A body meant for sacrifice. Just a little bit of a thing, at first glance a young girl, on the verge of sexual maturity. He could never be with her and not fantasize about having her in his lap, doing what was forbidden and yet perfectly acceptable. She was thirty years old.

"Donahooie. You visiting me or doing a wash?"

His mind had been wandering. To get some respite, he'd been staring at a sign, REMEMBER THE DROUGHT, DON'T WASTE WATER. There wasn't a drought and that's why nobody paid attention to signs anymore. You couldn't believe them. What the world needed was fewer signs or more up-to-date signs. Fewer would be better. He said, "Official business."

She looked at him with her Chinese eyes. "You got some identification?"

Donahoo moved Clancy's laundry along the table she was working at so they were out of Cominsky's line of sight. It was mostly bras and panties and ankle socks. As far as he knew, Clancy had only one skirt, which she was wearing now, a short, tight, black leather job, and no blouses, just the bulky blue jean jacket that was her trademark on El Cajon Boulevard. She was wearing it now too but it wasn't covering much. The zipper was hooked at the bottom and not pulled up.

Clancy palmed the hundred-dollar bill he had put in a sock. "What's this for?"

"Cominsky. You think you could put him outa his misery?"

Clancy glanced toward the window. She thought about it for a moment while she folded the bill. She shook her head and handed it back.

Donahoo pushed it away. "I'm looking for a guy named Willie Johnson."

Clancy made the money disappear. "You're still looking."

"He's an ex-Navy SEAL," Donahoo said, glancing around. The only other customer was an old lady measuring detergent and mumbling something to herself. She didn't appear to be listening. "He used to live on the hill. I've got reason to think he's back."

"Never heard of him."

"A Navy SEAL?" Donahoo got another hundred out of his pocket. "Willie Johnson, he's like Whoopi Goldberg, Clancy. He makes it off the hill? He becomes somebody? He's a hero." He waggled the bill. "Everybody remembers a hero."

Clancy went back to folding her clothes. Her voice was a whisper. "They never knew him, they'd still remember him."

"Of course," Donahoo said. "He gave lie to the myth. He proved you can get off."

"Then why would he come back?"

Donahoo made a helpless gesture. He didn't know that Willie Johnson was back on Golden Hill. He was just guessing. If he was Willie, and fucking up, it would just be a natural thing to do, he thought. Come home, even though his parents were dead, his brother and sister gone, his home boys doing time in Chino. There was a certain security in familiar surroundings.

"Is he in trouble?"

"Not yet," Donahoo said. "Ongoing investigation." He waited for her to turn around but she didn't. "I won't know until I find him."

"It must be important. You throwing hundreds around."

"I'm in a hurry."

She finally turned. A wisp of hair was in her face. She stuck out her lower lip and blew it out of the way. Donahoo loved the lip. He could practically stand on it.

"So what is it?" he asked. "Can you help me? I just need a lead. The name of a friend. An old haunt. Something."

"No."

"A scrap."

"No."

Donahoo gave her the other hundred and walked out. He wasn't used to paying for no information and he wasn't quite sure why he had done it but it had seemed like the right thing to do. He stole a last glance at Clancy. She was watching him. She didn't smile or wave. He got in the van.

Cominsky said, "What did you get?"

Donahoo said, "Three thousand Ivy," which was an address he'd already had going in, the last known residence of Willie Johnson's father, Walter Johnson.

"How much?" Cominsky asked. He got out his book. He was the accountant.

"Two hundred."

Cominsky wrote it down. "That's a lot of money for an address."

Yes, it was, Donahoo thought. But he had always liked Clancy, she had a couple little boys to raise, all on her own, and there had been previous occasions when he hadn't paid her enough, vis-a-vis the information she had provided, and there was a good chance he might not be around to make amends. There also was the time, this was way, way back, when they first met, Clancy had wanted to do him and he'd said no, on account of his being a cop. Donahoo thought that kind of disappointment must have been hard on the girl and probably still was. A couple hundred in no way assuaged that, but it did show some sensitivity.

"You said hello?" Cominsky asked.

Donahoo thought he must be losing it. He was screaming dreaming. "Oh, yeah."

chapter 7

Golden Hill was like Clancy Holden, a mix. Parts of it were okay, but there were others where you had to watch out. The west slope had a scattering of fine old homes, including some of the city's earliest mansions, now historic landmarks. There also was a section of substantial and still quite respectable Craftsman houses from the early 1900s. But much of the hilly, canyon-laced neighborhood was in decay, overwhelming the occassional rehab attempt.

Donahoo took the van through the bars-on-the-windows sections. He could have avoided them, taken a safer route through the municipal golf course or skirted Balboa Park, but that would have meant acknowledging the fear he felt, that somebody was waiting to do him harm.

The Mexican influence was becoming more pronounced. 99¢ D'TODO, Tortilleria Sinaloa. He went by vacant buildings and shuttered shops, a faded sign that said, OPENING SOON, past businesses that operated out of homes, advertising MOWERS SHARPENED and BIKES FIXED. He passed Brooklyn Elementary, which, apparently in anticipation, was painted completely with artful grafitti. This was pure Golden Hill now. Food Bowl, California Liquor, Heart 2

Heart Penny Smart Thrift. Sparky's and Snippy's and Studio Maureen and the door of beads that hung in front of Woody's, The Shop. New Visions Prestige Real Estate.

Cominsky said, "Here's what it says about kale," and proceeded to read, " 'Kale, if you wanta be hale.' "

"Not now," Donahoo growled.

He took Fern to Ivy. There was a Victorian on the corner, a fine old house, lots of rococo, a mansard roof. It would date back to when the hill really was golden. Donahoo liked it right away. It was painted lime green with a yellow trim. An 0 had fallen off the address, which read, 30 0.

"This is it?"

Donahoo nodded. He drove past and parked a short distance down the block. He checked the load in his Python.

"You think he's here?"

"No," Donahoo said. He pushed out. "What I want you to do is go around back of the house and wait there. If Willie comes out, ask him to hang around, I want to talk to him, okay?"

"Got it."

Donahoo looked at his watch. "I'll wait until you're in position."

"Right."

Cominsky went flapping down the street. Donahoo stood waiting. He hoped he was wrong about Willie. If a guy can get off the hill, if he can become a Navy SEAL, why in the hell would he turn to a life of crime? It didn't make sense.

There was the sound of gunfire. One shot, two. Oh, shit. Cominsky?

Donahoo ran for the house with the Python out. The door was locked. He kicked it in and entered, crouched low, fanning the Python.

The house was vacant. No furniture. Nothing.

Donahoo went from room to empty room. There was a mattress on the floor in one of them. That was it.

"Sarge!" Cominsky yelled, from somewhere out back.

Donahoo shouted, "Stay put! You okay?"

"Yes!"

Donahoo went into the kitchen. Willie was sprawled in a pool of blood next to a toy gun. He'd been shot twice in the head. He was dead.

"Cominsky!" Donahoo shouted. "Watch for somebody! We've got a fresh kill here!"

He went out the back. There was no sign of anyone. He checked both sides of the house. Nothing.

"Cominsky? Anybody in the alley?"

"No!"

Donahoo went blank. He didn't know how anybody could disappear that fast or which way they'd go. He just knew that they were gone. He got out his cellular.

How the hell did this happen? he wondered. Willie was an ex-SEAL. He wouldn't get nailed so easily by a stranger. The killer had to be someone he knew and trusted. A friend or accomplice.

And the toy gun? No SEAL was going to have that in his possession. So it had to be left by the killer. But why?

Oh, fuck, Donahoo thought. What if the killer had seen him arrive with Cominsky? What if the killer had watched as they parked down the block? What if . . .

The rest was a nightmare. Homicide sent two detectives Donahoo didn't know very well, Vickers and Dugan. Vickers mentioned several times that Willie's gun was a toy and anybody could tell it was from about a hundred yards. Dugan noted that the murder weapon, or what appeared to be the murder weapon, since it was recently fired, looked as if it could be easily traced. It was a .25 Beretta. All the serial numbers intact. Dugan brought it in from the side of the house, where a police dog, named Judy, had located it, shoved into a drain tile.

Vickers, smelling blood, said, "Sergeant, did you ever see this gun before?"

Donahoo, because there was no use lying, said, "Yeah, it's mine."

And Cominsky, who had been out looking around on his own, came in and announced, "This place is a compost heaven."

chapter 8

Everybody had their own version. They were in Saperstein's office telling how they saw it, and, since some of them hadn't seen it, how they didn't. Donahoo and Cominsky, Vickers and Dugan, Lewis.

"Here's how it happened," Donahoo said, giving his version for the third time. "I told Cominsky to go around back, down the block, into the lane. I said I'd wait until he got into position. Then I heard the two shots, so I went inside and found Willie. Period."

Vickers gave his version, which was also Dugan's version. He was a fat guy with frog eyes and pinched features and a small mustache that grew up his nose. He wore a porkpie hat and thought he was Popeye Doyle in *The French Connection*. Lewis had told him at one point to sit on the hat, and he did. He was that kind of guy, difficult.

"How about Donahoo didn't wait?" Vickers suggested. "He's a showboat. That fits. He goes in, the Python in his holster, the Beretta in his pocket. Two-gun Tommy."

Donahoo stirred but Lewis put out a warning hand.

"Willie shows his toy weapon. Donahoo, gut reaction, pulls the Beretta, bang, bang. Then he realizes what he's done. He yells to Cominsky, 'Stay put!' He has just enough time to hide the Beretta before he's gotta connect with Cominsky. Then he's gotta leave it in the drain 'cuz Dugan and I are just a few blocks away when the call comes in. We get there before he can break away to stash it somewhere safer."

Donahoo was still looking at Lewis's upraised hand. "Maybe somebody should read me my rights?" he said sarcastically.

Dugan was another fat guy, but better looking than Vickers, with elegant features, dark skin, and silver hair. He said, "I'm sorry, Tommy. It works for me."

"Bullshit, it's a frame," Lewis complained, giving his version, which was also part of Donahoo's version, except that Donahoo didn't know how this part worked yet. "It's got Mad Marvin's prints all over it."

Dugan wasn't buying. "The Beretta's got Donahoo's prints all over it."

"It's my gun," Donahoo said, trying to remain calm, but his mind was racing. He had never been treated like a criminal before. It was unnerving. "That's not in dispute."

"But you didn't take it in the house? And you didn't fire it?"

"No."

"And you don't know how it got in the drain pipe, newly fired?"

"No."

"You're still saying the last time you saw it was in a drawer in your apartment? Last Thursday?"

"Yes."

"And you can't say it was stolen, but that's the only way it could have left the place?"

"Yes."

Cominsky spoke for the first time. Donahoo knew it was difficult for him. The guy was in love, for chrissake. He was going to put Clancy in the mix, and, by doing so, he was going to make it stickier for him, Donahoo. "Clancy Holden also figures in this," Cominsky said. "She gave us the address."

Vickers struck like a fat snake. "What address?"

"The address of the house." Cominsky could hardly choke out the words. "Maybe she was setting us up?"

"She sent you there? To the Victorian?"

"Yeah."

Dugan was writing it down. He said, "Clancy? As in Irish? That's her first name?"

Cominsky, torn, said, "As in gorgeous."

Vickers looked at Donahoo. He was smiling slightly. "What? A hooker?"

Donahoo nodded. It was getting worse. Vickers and Dugan were going to talk to her. She was going to say it wasn't true. That she didn't give him the address, that she didn't give him anything.

Dugan had his pen poised. "Oh, yeah? Where can I find her?"

"El Cajon Boulevard."

"Can you be more specific?"

"Texas Street."

"Tell me how the frame works," Saperstein said to Lewis. "The frame vis-a-vis the time frame. Mad Marvin gets mad at Donahoo on Sunday. He fucks him on Monday. A very complicated, fast fuck. Who is that fast?"

Vickers said, "Superman."

"Later," Lewis told Vickers. He pulled up his pants and indicated Donahoo. It was all in the same motion, nothing wasted. "You wanta kill this guy, Vickers? There's no hurry, okay? He's been here twenty years. He's not going anywhere." Lewis turned to Saperstein. "Mad Marvin got mad at Tommy three months ago. That's when Tommy made him. That's plenty of time to cook this shit."

Vickers, undaunted, said, "How would Mad Marvin know it was Tommy who made him?"

"If he wanted to find out, he could."

"Maybe."

"Not maybe. Yes."

"It's possible," Saperstein conceded. "Let's look at it. Take it to its conclusion. Mad Marvin starts putting this together three months ago, but for a different purpose, he just wants to fuck Tommy over. Now, yesterday, he's got a different reason, a murder rap, and so he orders the frame to go ahead . . ." Saperstein was losing track of where he was going. "Why? Is it still only revenge? Or does it somehow help him?"

Donahoo knew the answer to that. He knew it back in the kitchen of the lime green Victorian. He said, "It helps him. Now he can kill me and make it look like one of Willie's home boys did it."

"See?" Lewis said, looking relieved. "It all makes sense. We're dealing with a twisted mind. One fell swoop, Donahoo is a disgraced cop, shooting an innocent guy, and what kind of witness, *sole witness*, to a murder is that? And when, in retaliation, Donahoo gets bumped off, it's by one of Willie's anguished friends, not Mad Marvin, who, conveniently, is in jail." Lewis looked around. He was excited. "I think it's perfect."

Vickers said, "I think it sucks."

Donahoo said, "So do I."

Saperstein picked up his phone. "Millie? Get me the DA." He was looking at Donahoo. "What I think we've gotta do is have you make a deposition, on video. That way we've got your testimony if something happens to you."

"And we'll want to talk to you some more," Vickers added, rising. He was getting his porkpie. "Like why are you looking for Willie in the first place? Just because he's an ex-Navy SEAL he blows up a sloop. I don't think so. We'll see you downstairs."

Cominsky, alarmed, said, "Isn't this for Internal Affairs?"

Vickers, looking directly at Lewis, said, "Not the way I see it."

Donahoo couldn't believe it was getting so out of hand. He had never panicked under fire in his life. Mostly, he'd shot guys in the knee. In his whole career there had been only one fatal shooting. He was suddenly acutely aware of the clutter of antiques in Saperstein's office, the Sheraton-style armoire, the Windsor bow-back chair. It used to be that Saperstein had a very spare office to demonstrate that the police department's budget ought to be spent on the street, not on executive trappings. Now, though, it was starting to look like a salon or something, and Saperstein was starting to look like a banker, there'd be a homburg next. The antiques were Saperstein's wife's idea, they didn't belong in what was once an austere office with just the beat-up filing cabinets and cheaply framed diplomas, awards and citations. There used to be a sofa and rubber tree plant instead of the dumb antiques. They didn't belong, and he didn't belong either, Donahoo thought. He should get the hell out. There was no comfort level.

"Uh, Tommy," Lewis said. He was hurting. "I think you should talk to a lawyer."

Saperstein was on the phone to the DA. "Hello, Davis?"

chapter 9

Donahoo went banging out of the police station. Sonofabitch, he couldn't believe Vickers, couldn't believe Dugan. Their minds weren't just closed, he thought, they were fucking *locked*. The dumb bastards actually presumed he had somehow lost it in a confrontation with Willie Johnson. That, or—something else they probably suspected— he had it planned all along. They were a jump ahead of everybody. They already had him convicted and sentenced.

See a lawyer, huh? Well, maybe he ought to, Donahoo thought. Who else was left to see? Lewis had ruined him for O'Malley. There were some things that O'Malley did, small habits, little idiosyncrasies, that had seemed innocent in the past but which now loomed suspect. Patting him on the knee, for example. O'Malley was a patter.

He felt a sudden twinge of sympathy for anybody caught up in the justice system. The cards stacked against them. Nobody they could really trust. Lawyers and priests. It had to be tough.

It was tough.

He headed for his Toronado which was parked on G Street. He tried to look on the bright side. One benefit of the frameup, he didn't feel like a target now, somebody waiting with a sniper's rifle. The frame had bought him some working space. There was a natural progression here. He had to be charged with murder or at least subjected to departmental discipline. Some action that would publicly brand him as Willie Johnson's killer. Then, once that was established, there would be the second stage, which called for some sort of underworld justice. It was then that he should start worrying about a sniper again.

Borrowed time? No, actually he had earned it, he thought, and now he should put it to good advantage. He ought to run with it. Dugan and Vickers weren't the only guys with a suspect. He had two of them. Mad Marvin Molino, he was prime. Prescott Havershot III, he was a possibility, however remote.

Donahoo tried to think of ways to make something happen. Molino was issuing very specific death threats. Maybe someone ought to threaten him? Tell him, hey, don't worry about the trial, you won't live for it either. Havershot was throwing his weight around. Maybe somebody should give him some diet advice.

He thought those were two really bad ideas, and also that he ought to follow through on them. Sometimes a bad idea was better than none. He couldn't just sit still. Vickers and Dugan were busy fashioning a noose. If he didn't keep moving they'd drop it on him, and his head would fit neatly inside. So the idea—this was now a good idea—was to keep moving.

He picked his way through a group of homeless men rearranging themselves on the sidewalk by the Sally Ann rehab center. They'd been in the sun and now they wanted the shade. It was going to be a warm afternoon. None of them asked for anything. He came this way often and they knew he was a cop. He felt guilty, as he always did. The conventional wisdom was that if you gave them money, they'd spend it on liquor or drugs. But what if some of them really were hungry and really would buy food? The solution would be to make sandwiches and hand them out. He never did that though.

"Sarge!"

Donahoo refused to look back. He picked up the pace. He didn't want any more questions until someone read him his Miranda rights.

"Wait!!"

Cominsky caught up, breathless. He panted, "Sarge, listen, I know what you were trying to do back there, but you didn't have to do it."

Donahoo finally looked at him but kept moving. "Huh?"

"Protect my feelings."

"I wasn't trying."

"If that's the kind of girl she is, it's best I know now, not later."

"I wasn't trying."

"It would be harder later."

"Cominsky," Donahoo said. "Listen to me. Clancy didn't give me the address. She didn't set me up. She didn't give me anything. Nothing."

Cominsky stared at him. "Then what about the two hundred bucks?"

"I was feeling generous."

"Huh?"

Donahoo had to stop. They had arrived at the Toronado. "It was a gift."

Cominsky went kind of blank. He was suddenly overloaded, processing stuff that didn't compute. He stammered, "But you charged it to the snitch fund?"

Donahoo made a helpless gesture. Yes, he'd done that, but it evened out. You took a little here. You put a little there. It was okay as long as you didn't take any for yourself.

"So how did you know where to go?"

"To the Victorian? Prior investigation."

"You were going there all along?"

"Yes."

Cominsky's face creased with a sloppy grin. It held for just a moment and then he got another thought. Donahoo knew exactly what he was thinking. If he, Donahoo, had lied once, he could lie twice. Cominsky was thinking that maybe he hadn't given the two hundred to Clancy.

"Uh," Cominsky said, stricken. "Sarge. If you needed the money . . ." He was having real trouble with it. His eyes were suddenly wet. "Why didn't you ask me?"

"I beg your fucking pardon?"

"What's going on?"

Donahoo thought that they were all doing it. Vickers, Dugan, Saperstein in a way, now Cominsky. They were jumping to conclusions. They were convicting him without a trial. All he had was Lewis, who thought he needed a lawyer.

He said, "*Et tu,* Cominsky?"

"What?"

"Okay, let's keep it simple: Fuck you."

He pushed away. He had to get somewhere by himself and think. What was going to save him, he thought, wasn't a lawyer, wasn't a priest, it was a cop. A cop who could figure out who really killed Willie Johnson.

At the moment he was the only cop he knew who wanted to do that and who could do that.

Maybe.

He drove over to Fifth Avenue, to Lee's, the cheapest restaurant in the Gaslamp, and bought half a dozen fried egg sandwiches, toasted, on brown. He got them for four-fifty. Five, with the tip. Not a tip. He just didn't wait for the change.

He drove back to the Sally Ann. He only got three takers for the sandwiches. He ate one of the leftovers and put two aside for Cominsky's compost.

chapter 10

American Steel. It used to be a big company with a lot of smelters. Now it was just a holding company and nobody knew what it held. Not for sure, anyway. Donahoo remembered reading that somewhere. It summed up his total knowledge of the fortune he was allegedly hunting.

The phone book said American Steel was in the Spreckles Building, an aging but still splendiferous marble-faced theater/office complex on Broadway in downtown San Diego, a block down and across from the venerable U.S. Grant hotel.

Donahoo parked on Front Street and walked back wondering if he was doing the right thing. It seemed kind of impulsive. He hadn't thought it out. Wasn't sure where he wanted it to go or how he wanted to take it.

The thing, of course, was to try to find out if Havershot had anything to do with him being framed for Willie Johnson's murder. Or, to the put it the way it had come to him, was the guy a screamer or a schemer? That was the question, and it had to be posed. The other question was how to do that.

He still didn't know when he arrived at the Spreckles. He stood under the blank marquee, looking through the row of heavy glass doors across the vast, high-ceilinged lobby with its intricate white-tiled floor to where a distant and very proper concierge stood guard. Double-breasted blazer. Bow tie.

He wondered. Should he or shouldn't he? He had the sudden wild thought—he was being contrary because she was expressly off-limits—that he might someday wish to marry Travata. So it wouldn't pay to piss off his future father-in-law. Not too much, anyway. What to do?

Havershot made up his mind for him. He suddenly appeared—from the underground parking garage, apparently—and started across the lobby for the elevators. He seemed to be in a hurry, walking with quick, determined steps.

Donahoo pushed inside and started after him. He was at a distance and thought he should call out. Havershot was already at the elevators. A door opened and he stepped inside.

"Pardon me," the concierge said, "You'll have to sign in," and the elevator door closed.

"Uh," Donahoo said, and the elevator door opened.

"It's okay, Charlie," Havershot told the concierge. "I'm acquainted with Sergeant Donahoo. I can vouch for him." He was obviously displeased but he was holding the door open. He was doing his best. He was under control. "Coming up?"

Donahoo joined him. A tall, thin, nicely arranged man with wide shoulders and long arms and big hands. An intelligent narrow face hung from a large forehead. Chiseled features and an interesting if somewhat petulant mouth. The Aryan brute barely contained. He'd be considered handsome if it wasn't for the slow eye. Donahoo wondered if they could ever be friends. Probably not.

"I don't suppose there is any chance of this being a coincidence?"

"No."

"Well," Havershot said. He was dressed in a dark gray business suit that was inappropriate for the changed weather. He looked like he'd be happy to get out of it. Maybe that explained the rush. He pushed a button, the fourth floor. "I assume the chief has had a talk with you? You'll have something to say as a result? Normally, I like an appointment, but seeing as it's you . . ." A smile flickered and died. "We can speak in my office."

"Yes."

The wheezing cage climbed slowly. Donahoo wondered what smelled musty, the building or Havershot. Up close, not in a rage, he looked older, world-weary. His pale blue eyes were listless. His breathing seemed shallow and slightly labored.

"You have five minutes."

"Whatever."

The elevator stopped at the fourth floor. Havershot got off and Donahoo followed him into a wide hall with windows looking out onto the theater's domed roof. The upper floors of the building formed a square around it. They turned a corner and then went only a few steps to a door with a frosted glass pane. AMERICAN STEEL. ENTER.

Havershot again led the way. An older, faded woman was sitting at a small wooden desk surrounded on all sides by old-fashioned metal filing cabinets. There was just the one stiff chair for a visitor. Nothing on the walls except a business license.

"Anything interesting?" Havershot asked the woman. She shook her head no. He took several messages off a spike. Thumbed through them impatiently. Put them in his pocket. "I don't want to be disturbed."

There was a second door with a frosted glass pane, the one word, PRIVATE. Havershot opened it and went in first. It was another office, larger than the reception area, but not by much. A floor-to-ceiling safe took up most of the wall behind the desk. It came with the place and would go well with Saperstein's antiques. The windows facing the building's corespace offered a view similar to that coming off the elevator. The theater roof.

"The street side is too noisy," Havershot said, seeming to sense Donahoo's unspoken question, and then, "Sit down."

Donahoo took one of the two stiff chairs. Havershot went behind his scarred oak desk and settled into an oak swivel of the same vintage. The only reasonably new things were the computer deck, scanner, copier, and phone/fax/message center. There was also an enormous paper shredder.

Havershot was to the point. No preliminaries. "Which is it? An apology or a promise?"

Donahoo wished it were that easy. He wanted to explain. He wanted to understand. Those two things at least. But a lot more. He also wanted his fears allayed. Say it isn't so, twit. Tell me you're not a threat. Tell me you're just a loudmouth.

"Speak up."

Jesus. Donahoo wondered if Havershot was for real. He also wondered if American Steel was for real. He was confused by the office's bare minimum setup. No, make that baffled, he thought. What was it they used to call it? Stark contrast? This was in stark contrast to Havershot's magnificent digs in Rancho Santa Fe. Very much so. And the contradiction didn't make any sense.

The phone rang in the outer office. There was a brief, muffled conversation and then a light rap on the door.

Havershot began, "I don't . . ." but the faded woman opened the door anyway.

She looked in and said, "It's Cardiff."

"Alright." Havershot picked up his phone and listened for several moments. He looked only once at Donahoo, at the end, when he said, "I'm not interested in the details, just get it done, Mr. Marvelous. *Do it, okay?*" He hung up. "I'm waiting."

"Yes," Donahoo said. He tried to get comfortable and couldn't. Well, here goes, he thought. He wasn't very hopeful. But this was something he had to do. He had to stand up to the sonofabitch. He didn't have very much but he liked to think he still had his self-respect. "I didn't get the chance to explain a few things the other night. First, I'm not interested in your money. Second, I'm not interested in Travata, or at least not yet, I just met the girl. Third . . ."

Havershot waved a big hand impatiently. He was starting to get angry. "What has this got to do with anything?"

"Well. You seem to be laboring under a misunderstanding."

"No." Havershot shook his head. It looked like he might lose it again. "This is what I told your police chief. The misunderstanding is on your part. What you don't understand is that Travata is emotionally unstable. What you don't understand is that I don't want you going anywhere near her."

"Yeah," Donahoo told him. "I understand that. But what *you* don't understand is, I didn't plan anything here, okay? It wasn't intentional. We're talking about a chance meeting. When I took her home, I didn't know who she was, and I didn't know who you were, and I didn't know anything about American Steel. So what I'm saying . . ."

"That's hardly the point."

"It is. Have you asked her? I walked into this blind, for chrissakes. You're screaming at a complete innocent. A babe in the fucking woods."

"I'm not screaming."

"You were the other night."

Havershot angrily waved his hand again. This time it was a gesture of dismissal.

"What the hell's the matter with you?" Donahoo demanded. "Don't you get it? There's no premeditation involved. I repeat, chance meeting. If I don't know about your money, how can I care about your money? So I resent—very much resent—you thinking that I do." He stopped to get his breath. "Something else I resent. Throwing your weight around with the chief. That's a bullshit thing to do. We've got a personal problem here—not a departmental problem. You're not gonna fix it talking to my superiors. You fix it talking to me."

Havershot reached for his phone. "Would you like me to call the chief again?"

Donahoo knew it was wrong as soon as he said it. "Would you like me to see Travata again?"

Havershot put the phone aside. He had a look of disgust. "I know your type. You stalk innocent, vulnerable women. You get them in your clutches. You dig in your dirty fangs and you won't let them go."

"Are you serious?"

Havershot fumbled in his desk drawer. His answer was a snarl. "You're an animal."

Donahoo started to push up. He was so angry he didn't see the gun until it was pointed at him, an exotic looking, eight-round Italian Mateba .38 Special.

"Last warning," Havershot said coldly. "If you ever go near my daughter again, you're a dead man, understand? That's the way it is. No discussion. No negotiation. No second chance. I'm just going to bury your ass and your dick along with it."

There was a click. Safety off.

"You know," Donahoo said. "Now I'm pissed. I came here to explain and maybe even apologize. I shouldn't have been in your house like that. I thought you were making a snowman somewhere—where were you supposed to be—Minnesota? That's not an excuse. But you're acting like a real jerk. You think you can order me around? Tell me what I can't do? If you weren't Travata's father, I'd kick the shit outa you."

"Get out of here," Havershot shouted.

Donahoo was boiling. "My five minutes are up?" He thought about going for the gun and decided he'd never make it. He was looking into Havershot's pale blue eyes, alive now with fury and, oddly, resignation. Well, he'd found out something, Donahoo thought. He'd seen that over-the-muzzle look before. The guy was capable of murder.

He backed out. The faded woman smiled good-bye.

He asked, "Who's Mr. Marvelous?"

She answered, "I'm afraid I never met him."

chapter 11

Donahoo wondered if maybe he should go home to bed. If he persisted, what was going to happen, probably, was that Mad Marvin Molino was going to get the drop on him too. It looked like that kind of day.

He found a pay phone. There was a guy he knew, an FBI Special Agent, William Galloway, and a quiet place he knew, Embarcadero Marina Park.

"Wild Bill? It's Tommy. The usual place. High noon."

They'd be talking about Molino, but Donahoo didn't say that, and Galloway didn't ask. He didn't have to. He could read the paper. They might also discuss Havershot, but Donahoo didn't tell Galloway that either. The less said the better. There were rumors the FBI was tapping itself.

The park was up on a knoll where they held the Pop concerts, there was a wide-angle view of San Diego Harbor, from the Tenth Avenue Terminal, tucked under the Coronado Bridge, to halfway around North Island Naval Air Station.

Some old men were feeding ducks. No old women, just old men. Donahoo wondered about that. Wondered why he hadn't thought to bring a bag of bread himself. Everybody ought to have some crust tucked away somewhere, he thought. Even him.

He found a bench to wait on. He plopped down and became a part of the picture. It seemed to have been painted by a nostalgia-bent marine artist who had captured things the way they were for the purpose of how they should be remembered. That kind of for-the-record detail.

Ships were fitted in all over, Navy and merchant marine, pleasure, all shapes and sizes, glistening in the sun, dazzling. Old wharves sagged and vacant buoys sulked. Donahoo gave an imaginary kaleidoscope a pretend twist. A new picture fell into place. The water was painted a solid flat gray. The sky was a cheery dinnerware blue. White sails snapped. Pelicans cruised.

Jesus, Donahoo thought. He was waiting for Galloway, but he wished he was waiting for Travata. It was a pleasant, sunny day, meant to be enjoyed, cherished, a respite between Pacific storms. The puddles drying in the road would be filled again before they emptied. The next rain was due that night, and two more storms were in the tube. It was abnormal. The wettest March ever. The Escondido reservoir was a foot and a half above the top of the dam. People were going up there to watch it spill over. You could see them on TV. One lady had said, "Who needs to go to Niagara Falls? We got it here."

An unmarked Plymouth showed up. Pale green and with an E for exempt plate. It parked in a puddle, and Galloway got out. He had two box lunches. They'd both be for him. He picked his way through the puddles. He approached like a loose balloon, sort of rolling along, very gentle for a hippo.

Donahoo looked at his watch. The guy was almost fifteen minutes late. Donahoo had learned something though, so it couldn't be called time misspent. He'd learned there were three ways to feed ducks: piecemeal, scatter, and dump. Piecemeal was when you presented scraps of bread one at a time. Scatter was when you flung a handful in a wide arc. Dump was when you ceremoniously emptied your bag all in one spot and caused a wild scramble.

Galloway made it to the bench. He put the two box lunches down. He turned and positioned himself for dining.

"The Mandarin Szechuan Buffet," he said, unwrapping chopsticks. He opened one of the boxes. His frog eyes grew larger, and he dug in. "You're back in the news, huh? Detective Ce-leb-ri-ty."

Donahoo didn't want to look. Two kinds of chicken, pork ribs, deep fried shrimp, a bunch of noodles, egg rolls. Ugh.

They had been on a case together, this was six years previously, a kidnapping that involved several jurisdictions, and Donahoo had bonded with Galloway. The guy liked women, he liked whiskey. Then he got in trouble. He was seeing a lady who got arrested in a porno bust and she started saying sensitive things that sounded like she got them from Galloway. He said it wasn't true but the Bureau was going to kill him anyway. So Donahoo (it didn't make any difference to him, just as long as it was solved) threw the kidnapping case solution to Galloway. He gave him the whole thing and made him a hero. *Man, you saved my life,* Galloway had said then, and it was true. Galloway got to keep his career, his wife and family, his house and his car and his sailboat. So Donahoo figured he was owed something.

"What do you know about Prescott Havershot III?"

"Nothing."

"There's not the slightest blip on your radar screen?"

"No blip."

"Okay. What do you know about Mad Marvin Molino?"

"The *Wasp*, she's going out," Galloway said, looking at the aircraft carriers docked across the harbor at North Island NAS. "I hear they're keeping the *Kittyhawk* till Easter. Did you hear that?"

"Do you think he's really mad?"

"They're going to hold a sunrise service on the deck, I can't believe that's allowed. The Resurrection, that's a Christian belief, not universally embraced. We're supposed to have separation of church and state. I don't think there should be sunrise service in the service."

Donahoo was watching an old man. He was a dumper. He had a large brown paper bag and he emptied it. The bread piled like a crust pyramid. He stomped away. The ducks attacked.

"How about if they held it at noon?"

"That would be okay."

Donahoo sighed. "Why I'm asking," he said. He turned to Galloway. Held his arm. Made him lower it. Forced him to put an egg roll back. "The guy says he's going to kill me. I wondered if the Bureau had a reading on that. It must have a shitload file on him. It watched his house for three months. It's gotta know something I don't know. I could use the help."

"Well," Galloway said. He was looking longingly at the egg roll. "I'm not all that privy. I don't know what the Bureau thinks and I don't know if it cares. If I were to guess, they'd happily let him kill you, you messed up a big case for them, you heard that?"

"Saperstein mentioned it. Briefly."

"Then what the hell . . ."

"He didn't give any details."

"And you want some?"

"Yeah."

"Sorry. They've got me in a cage in the basement. All I get is scraps, half truths, rumors. Wishful thinking."

Donahoo gritted his teeth. "You owe me."

"Take it easy." Galloway pulled out from Donahoo's grip. He retrieved the egg roll. He ate that and some more stuff. "When is this over?"

Donahoo said, "Never," because that's how much Galloway owed him.

Galloway said, "It's over when you die, Tommy."

"Is that gonna be soon?"

"It could be quick."

Oh? Donahoo wondered about the fates. Galloway was a blimp. He had clogged arteries. He was a candidate for a stroke/heart attack/sudden-death-on-the-toilet-seat syndrome. He was going to cave in on himself from sheer weight, or he was going to burst—his skin was going to give way—there was going to be an implosion or an explosion. There was no way, in the normal course of events, that Galloway could outlast him, Donahoo. But all that had changed.

"Is he nuts?" Galloway asked, as if talking to himself. He was saying things Donahoo already knew. "It's hard to tell. Molino, there's this terrible anger in him, this incredible rage, it can surface without warning, but I don't know that makes a guy crazy, maybe he's just got a bad temper? Is he capable of killing you? Of course. He's a killer, for chrissakes. Has he still got the organization for it? Absolutely. That hasn't changed. He's in The Mob. Is he dumb enough to go after a cop, knowing that's probably gonna make things tougher for him in jail, even if there's no proof he had you snuffed? Now you've got me. I don't know. There is dumb and there is dumber. What I think, it's dumb to be in The Mob, with less effort, you can be in the FBI, run the whole fucking Justice Department." Galloway put aside his first box. It was empty. He opened the other. "Think about it. Who did Janet Reno ever have to kill to get made?"

Donahoo thought he'd leave that alone. He said, "Is there a point? Do you know anything?"

"The talk is it was a gambling case," Galloway said, lowering his voice, even though there was nobody to overhear. "Conspiracy. Major crime figures. Professional and college ball. Some sort of reorganization or takeover at the national level. A few key players to be eliminated. Players, not athletes. Don't misunderstand."

"Fuck. I honestly don't."

"People were coming out here to talk to Molino about how to do that. The Bureau was listening on bugs. They were talking in circles but their intentions were plain enough. There was going to be one more meeting, everybody, to get it finalized, and then you call the SWATs, no case. Months of work go down the drain. Maybe years."

"All my fault?"

"They gotta blame somebody."

"Why not blame the Witness?"

"They did. But they can't hurt him. You, they can hurt."

Donahoo thought *fuck* some more. He wasn't learning anything. Except maybe how to trigger a depression. He thought he might be getting into one and that it might be clinical. Before this was over, he was going to need a doctor with a couch, a couple extra notepads. There was going to be an outpouring.

"You want miracles?" Galloway asked. "Pat answers? There aren't any. There are only suspicions." He seemed torn: The scallop or the sliver of lobster? He asked the question again. This time he wanted a different answer. "When is this over?"

Donahoo said, "Okay, last time, I'll never bother you again," and Galloway, choosing the lobster, answered in a whisper, "It looks like they're trying to make a deal."

"Who?"

"The Bureau."

"How?"

"Deviously."

Donahoo thought yeah, but he didn't see how that worked. The Witness's murder was a local case. It belonged to DA Davis, and the FBI didn't have any case, because he, Donahoo, had fucked it up for them.

"This is only what I surmise," Galloway said. "There are a lot of comings and goings. Big shots in from Washington. They've been talking to Molino at length. Not in the Detention Center, they're staying clear of it. They don't even have him at our offices. They take him to The Taxidermist, bring him over in chains. There is someone in these meetings who wants or needs to keep a low profile."

Donahoo found that interesting. The Taxidermist was an FBI front in the warehouse section of Little Italy. It was supposed to be a business but the sign on the door always said CLOSED. There was a big room in the back where they occasionally ran special operations.

"Secret talks?"

"Hush-hush."

"What about?"

"Again, what I surmise, I'm only guessing." Galloway's fat face beamed with pleasure. Donahoo wasn't sure if it was the scallop or the anticipation of being free from his debt. "A federal case would take precedence—if there was a federal case—but there isn't a federal case." More beaming pleasure. It was unseemly. "Yet."

Donahoo didn't like where this was going. He looked away. There were some Mexicans huddled quietly at a picnic table. One had a bicycle. They had their heads close together. They looked like they were plotting something. Donahoo could imagine the conversation: *'Did you bring your gun?'* He said, "Continue."

"There are two ways the Bureau can resurrect the case you blew for them. One, they don't need to make the case, Molino simply pleads guilty, implicates others, gets a light sentence, maybe even walks away. Two, secretly, so his crime associates don't know, he provides evidence, lets the Bureau make a case, but it is mostly against others, hardly nothing against him, and again he gets off easy, maybe walks."

"What about the Witness murder?"

"Lost in the shuffle. You're not listening. The federal case takes precedence. It could drag on for years. By the time it's over, Justice works out something with the local yokel, claiming it's in the national interest, and it's probably not DA Davis, it's somebody else, and it's not just over, it's all over."

Donahoo considered. There were four or six kids, all of whom belonged in school, fishing off the dock, unmindful of the warning sign. FISH FROM THE BAY MAY CONTAIN CHEMICALS KNOWN TO CAUSE CANCER AND BIRTH DEFECTS. EATING THESE FISH MAY BE A RISK FOR SOME PEOPLE.

May be a risk? Come on, guys, Donahoo thought. Can't you make the call? He said, "Interesting theory."

"Check it out," Galloway said. "They've got Molino over at The Taxidermist right now. They take him in and out the back door. You could go over and watch the alley. You could probably see them take him out. Or you could go watch over at the Detention Center. See them take him in. Look for a big black Cadillac."

"What's it prove?"

"That they're talking deal."

"Sure. But maybe not the deal you're talking."

Galloway found a largish prawn in his seafood medley. He said, "If you were Molino, what kind of deal would you be talking. Let's hear what works for you. It's different?"

"Okay. It's exactly like you've laid it out. So I should be happy? Molino takes a walk on the federal stuff and the Witness case gets shuffled into oblivion. He's free, so why hold a grudge?"

"The guy is crazy. He still wants your heart. What's the best time to kill you? When there's no reason left."

Donahoo thought that Galloway had him there.

chapter 12

A big black Cadillac. Donahoo stood waiting for it. He was propped against the wall of a custom birdcage manufacturer called ROOST-ABOUTS. A guy inside was singing, "Canary me back to ol' Virginee..." Donahoo thought this might be a front too. He was pretending to be waiting for somebody in the shop. He kept looking at his watch, looking in the window, and he was pretending to read the late street edition of the *Union-Tribune*.

The Taxidermist was across the street, on the corner, Beech and India, a sagging, peeling, two-story clapboard with the upstairs windows blanked out by whitewash. The downstairs display window, barred like the entrance, had a stuffed horse in it. A stuffed owl was in the saddle. The CLOSED sign was gone. There was a new one that said, SORRY WE MISSED YOU.

Donahoo fussed with the *Union-Tribune*. This was like old times. The FBI had run the kidnapping operation out of The Taxidermist. Twenty agents looking for a Japanese industrialist named Sango Hukaruzi, who had disappeared on a business visit to San Diego, and who (they thought) had been snatched by a Thai gang keeping him prisoner in Ocean Beach. Actually, he had fallen victim to a Mexican gang that was keeping him in Tijuana. The FBI thought money was the object. Wrong again. It was a patent. Digital camera stuff. The Mexicans didn't want it for themselves. They were just hired guns. Some Germans had wanted it.

Donahoo checked the time and looked in the birdcage shop. He didn't like being out in the open but he had to be if he was going to see anything. The alley that Galloway had mentioned wasn't an alley. It was a deep dead-end driveway. It actually served a side entrance, not a back door. It was a very constricted space.

If the Caddie showed up, if it went down the driveway, if it collected a guy who looked like Mad Marvin Molino—would that make Galloway right about them trying to make a deal?

Donahoo thought, *probably*. The guy couldn't be wrong all the time.

His cellular beeped. He wondered if he should answer it. Maybe Galloway with more information? Maybe Galloway with cold feet?

It was Cominsky. He said, "Sarge. T'ai Ch'i? Singing lessons? We've got to do something to divert our minds. We can't be just thinking shit all the time. It's not healthy."

Donahoo said, "Be an Herbalife distributor."

Cominsky sounded delighted. "Would you do that?"

The Caddie showed up. Donahoo clicked off. He turned toward the shop window, using it as a mirror in which he could watch. The Caddie came up from Pacific Highway, bumped over the railroad tracks on Beech, made the turn onto India, then turned again, this time into The Taxidermist's driveway.

Donahoo folded his paper and walked across the street. He kept out of line-of-sight until he was on the opposite sidewalk. Then he had to reveal himself to look down the driveway.

The Caddie had stopped at the building's side entry. Its rear driver's-side door was shoved open, and a large man in a dark blue suit emerged and held it. He turned and looked briefly at Donahoo. He held up a hand, meaning stay away. He turned back.

Donahoo waited a moment and then moved forward. He wanted a better, closer look. Molino came out of the building, his hands cuffed, his feet shackled. Two more beefy agents had hold of him, one on each side, clutching his arms. Molino looked tired, angry, and maybe a little sullen.

Yeah, a deal, Donahoo thought. They were trying to patch one together. They had to bring him here to talk to the cutters. They couldn't do it at the Hall of Justice Detention Center. The place was a sieve. A cutter couldn't work there. Somebody would recognize him. He'd show up in the morning and by the afternoon they'd know about it in The Mob. It was less risk to move Molino around, there were places he would be naturally going, to arraignments, bail hearings, attorney conferences. This could be one of those trips or meetings.

"Hey?!" It was the large man holding open the car door. He had glanced back and he was reacting in alarm. He was reaching into his coat. "Keep moving!"

Donahoo found himself staring into Molino's strangely empty eyes. They were like The Taxidermist's upstairs windows. They were blank.

"Motherfucker!" Molino shouted. He was suddenly struggling with the agents holding him. "What's this sonofabitch doing here? Keep him away from me!"

Donahoo had the same thought. Keep the crazy bastard in check. Molino was twisting violently. The agents were having a hard time restraining him.

"Keep him away!" Molino suddenly pulled free from his guards. He slammed the open car door into the spine of the man who was supposed to be holding it. The man screamed and went down, dropping his gun, which he had just taken from his holster. Molino bent and scooped it up. He held it in both hands. He rammed it at the base of the man's skull. A 2-inch S&W Model 10 Snubby .38 Special.

One of the guards yelled, "Fuck," and the other got on a hand radio and said frantically, "Trojan. We've got a problem."

Donahoo moved down the driveway. He held his hands up, away from his body, shoulder height.

Molino said, "Motherfucker, stay back," and Donahoo belatedly realized what was happening: Molino thought that he, Donahoo, had come to kill him. It was the kind of thing Molino would pull. Preemptive strike.

Everybody was frozen.

"Relax," Donahoo said. "I just came to talk. I just wanted to tell you something."

Molino waited. They all waited. Especially the large man with the hard steel at the base of his skull.

"Don't do it," Donahoo told Molino, and he meant don't pull the trigger, and don't make a deal. "You don't have to do it. So don't do it. Just say no."

Molino hesitated. He had a clear shot at Donahoo. He just had to flick the gun up and pull the trigger. But if he did that he'd probably be killed a moment later. The agents behind him had their weapons drawn now.

"I could put a hole in your belly."

"Think first. Maybe you need me?"

"What the fuck you saying?"

"What I said. Don't do it."

"That's it?"

"Yes."

Molino considered. Donahoo imagined the wheels turning. Or, in Molino's case, grinding. In any event, a thought process, but there was no way of telling where it was taking them.

"Maybe we could talk about it sometime," Donahoo said. "Just you and me. Private."

Molino considered some more. He seemed to get the message and he seemed to like it. Maybe nothing definite was being promised but at least it got him off the hook now. He could back down and—if it was worrying him—not look bad.

"Okay?" Donahoo urged.

Molino tossed the Snubby at Donahoo's feet. Donahoo kicked it under the Caddie. It was all over.

The agent with the hand radio said, "You're Donahoo, aren't you?"

Donahoo showed him his ID, confirming it.

The agent said, "Well, what the fuck are we going to do about this?"

Donahoo said, "Forget it, I guess."

He turned around and left the driveway. Nobody said anything or tried to stop him. No harm done, or so they thought, and extra paperwork was always a pain in the ass, and handing a prisoner a gun wouldn't look good on their performance charts, so forget it.

He went back across the street and then down the block to where he had parked the Toronado. He felt a little shaky, but otherwise okay.

If the FBI had a deal in the making, perhaps he had put it on hold for a while, that was the best he could hope for. He had maybe bought himself a little time to come up with a better offer. Mad Marvin, what do you want most in this whole wide world, and what's the best way to give it to you?

Donahoo thought that he would put his mind to that after he figured what he had to give to Prescott Havershot III. He thought it was a pain having two guys gunning for him. Twice the work.

He liked the way the FBI used code names though. He thought maybe they ought to have some code names for Squad 5. Maybe he should put Cominsky to work on that. All they had was Spick and Spook. They needed some more.

'Trojan, we've got a problem.'

Gawd, how he liked that. It was wonderful. The guy could have been talking to a soldier or a prophylactic. Probably a prophylactic. Hey, Molino, you're the gambler, you want in on the action? This is a safe bet.

chapter 13

Donahoo went home, to Uptown and The Arlington. To a small studio with a narrow balcony that overlooked California 163 and the back of Balboa Park. To his cat, Oscar, and his Old Crow, and a record player with one record, *'I Wonder Who's Kissing Her Now.'*

He said hello to Oscar and put some Old Crow in a chilled glass, no ice. He wondered how he could spend a whole day just confirming things. Molino might kill him. Havershot might kill him. Hadn't he known that going in? So what had he accomplished?

Well, for one thing, he had demonstrated that he was getting old, he thought. He'd been caught out twice. By a Snubby and a Mateba. That made him wonder. Especially about the Mateba. It was an unusual gun to keep at the office. Not very suitable as a defensive weapon.

On his answering machine, Saperstein screamed: "You're jerking off the FBI? You're fucking with Havershot? Are you outa your mind?"

Lewis's voice: "Tommy. Come in. Surrender peacefully. You won't be harmed."

And Cominsky: "Sarge. Would you like to take a class with me?

We could learn massage. Hypnosis? Or we could learn to dance. There's an introductory offer, with or without partner, beautiful facilities, the Diamond Dance Club."

Donahoo put on the record. He sat down and thought about all the women in his life, now gone. His ex-wife, Monica, and his one sure love, Presh Logan, and the one who got away, Rosie The Snake G-string, the Wham Bam Ice Trail, and the one who was still running, Catalina De Lourdes Venezuela, and the one he had to throw back, Theresa Battistoni. You want young? She was young. She also was Cruz Marino's girl, and Cruz was hiding somewhere down in Mexico, and someday Cruz was going to kill El Presidente.

All in the past. No one in the present. Travata Havershot wasn't in his life, Donahoo thought. Not yet anyway, and probably not ever. Daydreams come and fantasies go, but it's hard to quarrel with a Snubby and/or a Mateba, especially when your Python is still in its holster.

He wondered if maybe there was something else he should be doing now. Maybe he should be looking for Clancy to brief her on Vickers and Dugan. He knew it was useless though. Clancy wouldn't lie for him or anybody else. She thought telling the truth was going to get her into heaven. It was what made her such a great snitch. She had religion.

> *I wonder . . . who's kissing . . . her now.*
> *I wonder . . . who's teaching . . . her how.*
> *I wonder . . . who's looking . . . into her eyes,*
> *Breathing sighs . . . telling lies.*

Donahoo couldn't quite figure his mood, so he didn't know who he should be thinking about, Monica or Presh, Rosie or Catalina. Normally he had to be pretty pissed to think about Monica. Down in the dumps to think about Presh. He was cynical when it was Rosie and hopeful with Catalina. He hoped she was okay. He hoped he might meet her again someday. Theresa? He was old.

He drank his bourbon and listened to the record, and after awhile he realized that he wasn't thinking about any of them. He wasn't pissed or down in the dumps or any of those things.

He was scared, and he was thinking of Travata Havershot, aka Jumpy.

He wasn't sure why he was scared. Was it because she was forbidden? Or was it because, even though forbidden, he was still thinking about her, and couldn't help himself?

He dug through various pockets until he found the slip of paper with Travata's pager number on it. It was unlisted, but he had ways. He'd had the number since Sunday, from a friend at the telephone company. He hadn't tried calling it yet.

Travata Havershot. Lifted shoe. Repressed heart. A soaring fuck and an emotional dust bin. An up and down lady, and if Mad Marvin could have started plotting three months ago, then Travata could have started three months ago, too. Maybe it didn't all begin when she limped into The Waterfront. Maybe it began . . . when?

Maybe, possibly, a long time ago, Donahoo thought, and he was beyond that now, struggling with the real question: Why? He looked at the phone. It was only a few feet and yet a million miles away.

Well, he sure had some kind of an apartment, Donahoo thought. He didn't see how he could possibly make it as far as that phone. Yet another stark contradiction. He found them all the time in killers. The guy's got a zillion brain cells and can't come up with a kind thought. That's what was happening out there. Try to explain it. Go ahead, try. Now as for size. There was something to say for the lady who didn't care how big it was as long as she knew she'd gotten laid. There was something to say for style. Donahoo thought that applied equally to his studio as it did to a criminal brain. The studio didn't qualify as an apartment. It was more the size of a smallish office, about the size of a budget-minded Saperstein's, or a stark-contradiction Havershot's. It had a bar kitchen fitted between a bookcase/entertainment center, a door to a shower-only bathroom, a Murphy bed, and a fireplace.

He had rented the place after his divorce from Monica, needing to save money, since he'd got hit for alimony while also contributing to the support of his wayward priest father, Charlie. Neither obligation existed anymore. Monica had found other means. Charlie was dead.

But Donahoo had opted to stay in The Arlington, clinging precariously to the canyon wall. The freeway winding below was noisy and dirty. But there were a lot of things that he liked. The unobstructed view of the semi-tropical jungle of Balboa Park. The balcony, the high ceiling, the fireplace that worked, the big Murphy that he never had to make, just lifted it into the wall and all excesses vanished.

I wonder . . . who's buying . . . the wine . . .
For those sweet lips . . . I used to call mine.
I wonder if she . . . ever tells him . . . of me.
I wonder . . . who's kissing . . . her now.

Donahoo pushed up and went to the fridge and got another chilled glass and another portion of Old Crow. He wondered how a guy might pass into another dimension where he didn't know doubt or fear. The best way to get there was to just go, he thought.

He found Travata's pager number again, dialed it, and left his number. He thought he was really kidding himself this time. If he looked in the mirror, and he wasn't going to do that, there would be this big craggy mug, a head that could be cast in bronze as a tribute to tough shanty Irish. Graying hair falling untamed over his collar, black bushy eyebrows, a dark jaw that wouldn't stay shaved. A busted nose and a no-nonsense mouth that got harder all the time. Blue eyes getting dimmer. They used to be the color of steel. Now they were aluminum. He was fast losing his charm.

What did the child see in him?

The phone rang. That quick.

Travata Havershot said, "I thought you'd never call," and Donahoo told her, finishing his Old Crow and putting the glass aside, "Neither did I."

chapter 14

He met her halfway. There was a place he knew, Vic's By the Beach, a sports bar in Encinitas. It wasn't by the beach, but it was close. It had twenty television sets and three guys named Vic. They walked around in bad dinner jackets and shook hands with people. They all claimed to be the owner. It was a dumb gimmick but it worked. The place was always packed. It also had great bread sticks.

She was sitting in a dark corner with a draft Bass ale. Wearing some sort of gaucho outfit. The black leather hat with the flat top and the broad brim and the drawstring under the chin. A fancy embroidered brown leather open vest over a long-sleeved buttoned-to-the-throat white blouse. A long, full black skirt and high, no-frills black leather boots. All she was missing was the whip and the spurs.

He was struck, again, as he was the first time, by her disconcerting beauty. Wonderful liquid green eyes that were almost too large for her face. A wide full mouth that also pushed the limit. An in-your-face bank robber's nose splattered with freckles. Banana blond hair, cut too short, worn too mussy. And attitude. It was as if someone had combined the best parts of an Irish elf and a Greek goddess. It was hard to explain, but a goddess wasn't perky, he thought. Travata was.

He said, "Hello."

She said, "I like your balls, Sergeant."

He thought, don't be too sure. He sat down like he was joining a keg of dynamite.

He had a very vaguely formed plan.

He was going to talk to her.

He was going to try to determine if she really was emotionally disturbed or if that was just Prescott Havershot's way of fending off undesirable suitors.

He was going to probe the theory that she might have known about him before The Waterfront, which might possibly make her a knowing, possibly an unwitting, accomplice to the Willie Johnson donkey fuck.

He was going to take his time and do it right.

He wasn't going to leap into anything.

"How'd you find out I was a cop?" he asked.

"Father," she said, digging into her gaucho purse, it looked like a saddle bag. She withdrew and unfolded a fax, which she pushed at him. "He says you're summa cum laudable. But that doesn't change his mind."

The fax was a report from a private investigator. Some things were blanked out (like who sent it). Others were highlighted (his age, his salary; his marital status, divorced). The citations were still intact. What made him so laudable?

Impressed, he said, "That was fast."

Taking the fax back, she said, "And expensive."

He wondered who had paid for it. She or Havershot? Now that she was suspect, he didn't trust anything about her. She was all high-risk.

"I honestly didn't," she said, smiling. "Think you'd call, I mean. After what Father said to you?" She reached across the table and squeezed his hand briefly. Her touch was electric. It was all he could do not to withdraw. His excuse was to sample her Bass. "Most men? They'd be scared off by something like that. They'd be in Pittsburgh by now. Still moving."

"Yeah, well," Donahoo said. "Sticks and stones." He looked

around for the help. He needed a real drink. Some of that old Old Crow. "What about you?"

"Me?"

"Did you get into trouble?"

She laughed. "No. There's nothing he can do to me. I'm a big girl now." She stopped, frowning. "Except kick me out of the house, of course. It's his house."

"And his money."

"Not exactly."

Oh? A waitress was looking their way. Looking but not seeing them. Vic's By the Beach was formerly a Boll Weevil hamburger joint, very dark inside, no windows. He waggled a hand.

"It's my money," she said.

"Yeah, tell me about that," Donahoo said, acting like he wasn't interested. He got his napkin and opened it up. He spread it out between them and flattened it. "How come you still live at home?"

She didn't answer. He glanced up from the napkin. She seemed hurt and angry.

"You being, you know, a big girl," he said. "Most young ladies your age are out on their own. They've got an apartment. They're in another city. They couldn't wait a moment longer than necessary. That's, uh . . ." He was going to say normal. He said, ". . . usual."

"What's so great about it?"

"Living alone?"

"Yeah."

"Well, for one thing, when you're entertaining, daddy doesn't kick down the door."

She grinned. That, for some reason, made her happy again.

"It's a small price to pay," she confided, leaning forward, lowering her voice. "Besides, it doesn't happen very often." She mussed up the napkin he had spread between them. "There's all kinds of places to do it. The only reason I took you home, I didn't know you, I wasn't sure about you, but I didn't think you'd pull anything funny in my house, okay? That was the only reason." She looked at him. "We don't have to do it there anymore. We can do it anywhere we want."

Yeah, Donahoo thought, on the moon. The weak gravity would be a boost. One giant leap for strange kind. He got the napkin straightened again. Without meaning it, he said, "My place?"

"Maybe someday."

He decided to keep pushing. It didn't matter, he thought. He could get up, and he could walk out. Anytime he wanted. It was his call. "Why not now? You're still not worried about me, are you?"

"A highly decorated police sergeant? Hardly."

"Then what's the problem?"

"You don't think it's a little boring?"

He was surprised. He wasn't sure how to answer. "Not with you."

She smiled in appreciation and showed him a key that had been in her hand all the time. It was a skeleton key and looked like it might open a closet door. It wasn't a motel key anyway. There was no tag.

"It's to this place I know," she said. "An old shed on the property next door to our house. They call it a barn but it's not a barn. It's a shed." She looked at him with crinkled eyes. "There is some hay in it, though."

Donahoo didn't think you could jump very high on hay. You'd probably sink. He said, "What's wrong with a motel?"

"There's no risk."

"Oh? Of what?"

"Getting caught."

Donahoo thought, Jesus Christ. What was wrong with her? "You *want* to get caught?"

"No, no," she said quickly. "I hate getting caught. What I like is the potential for it. The danger of it happening. That's what makes it exciting for me. It's like, you know, a forbidden act, and any moment someone may find you, stop you, and you won't, you know . . ." She was looking at him. She said, this time very slowly, "Achieve?"

"Oh."

Now she laughed and her hands flew apart in a kind of backward clap. "That's all!"

Well, Donahoo thought. He wished he had stronger information to go on here. He knew some retarded people weren't all that saddled with sexual inhibitions. But Travata wasn't retarded. He also knew there could be, *might* be, some validity to the emotional damage claim, but he hadn't seen any clinical evaluation. He just had Havershot's word, and if he trusted that, he believed in the tulip fairy. For the moment, until he got better evidence, he had to take the lady at face value, he thought. Okay, she liked to live dangerously, but so did a lot of other people, including himself, occasionally. He'd made the trip to Rancho Santa Fe. Maybe there was nothing really wrong with her. Maybe she just had a high sex drive?

He said, "Uh, I gotta ask you this, I'm still smarting from the old boy's fortune hunter crack, but it does raise a legitimate question: Why me? If you're an heiress . . ."

"What? I can only fuck an heir?"

"No. But you might wanta stick with your herd."

"Why?"

"I dunno. Isn't that usual? When I read the engagement notices, that's what it sounds like, a couple of good fortunes getting together."

"You read the engagement notices?"

"I read the lovelorn. I'm a cop."

"So what are you saying? You want to get engaged?"

"No. I want you to answer the question. You walk in a bar, you look around, you pick me. Why?"

She was silent for a moment. Looking at him strangely. "You really don't know?"

"No."

"A cop without a clue?"

"Yes."

She laughed. "You're probably not going to like this, but I think I just got lucky." Donahoo felt both complimented and put down. He thought he was getting into a no-win situation. He was drawing some very bad cards.

She was immediately contrite. She took hold of his hand again. "I'm sorry. This isn't easy for you, is it?"

"No," he admitted. He could think of easier things. Like shoving a watermelon up a dog's ass.

"It's the money?"

"Partly."

"Well, forget it," she said. "It's in a trust fund. I don't get it till

I'm thirty. Five years to go." She was still holding his hand. "Read my hips. You won't last that long. You'll be worn out."

Donahoo pulled away. He wondered who had set up the trust and why. He wished that he had had more time. He should have gone down to the public library, the California Room. Read up on the Havershots and American Steel.

"My grandfather," she said, sensing his question. "Prescott Havershot II. He and my father didn't get along. So while he left Father in control of the family fortune, it was within very rigid, enforceable guidelines. The trust must grow at a set rate annually. If it fails to do so it comes to me. So Father is always running, very hard."

Donahoo thought that was interesting. "Who keeps score?"

"A lawyer. Malcolm Philpott, of Herzog, Garfield and Philpott. He's a shark. He gets a fat bonus if Father defaults."

Donahoo wondered how fat. He also wondered what the trust was worth.

"Enough questions," she said firmly. She was watching him rearrange the napkin she had mussed. "Why don't you give up on that? They'll give you another one."

"My cat, Oscar," Donahoo explained. "He likes the bread sticks." Suddenly he felt like Cominsky the Gatherer. "I'm gonna wrap some up for him. If we ever get any." He looked for the waitress. She had disappeared. He wondered if he should complain to the Vics. He hadn't complained to anybody for a while.

"Your cat likes bread sticks? You're weird, you know that?"

"The cat is weird."

"No. You."

Donahoo looked at her. If anybody was weird, it was her, he thought. He was back on that again. He couldn't keep his mind made up. She kept changing it for him with everything she said or did. She was loose and she was tight, a very confusing combination. He wondered if maybe she was *on* the edge but not *over*? Could that be it? That would explain a lot of things. It might even explain everything. He also thought that if she was on the edge it was because she liked being there. Now, did this make her emotionally damaged?

"Are we gonna do it or not?"

Donahoo thought: *Big mistake.* He was drawing a blank and his resistance was crumbling. He felt like he was under attack by lust microbes. They were eating away at his last defense, his sanity.

"What's a girl got to do?"

He gave up. He wasn't getting anywhere being ignored in Vic's By the Beach. His career and life were in jeopardy, and only he could save it. He had to get hold of this wayward piggy bank and he had to shake her until the facts fell out.

The skeleton key got dumped into the gaucho bag. "You pick."

Donahoo looked at her. All his good intentions went out the door. They were out on the street. They were blocks away by now. They'd made it to the beach. They were gone.

"Well," he said. He left a five to cover the Bass. "You want forbidden? How about a crime scene? The yellow tape is still up. They catch us trespassing, they may shoot us."

She was looking at him expectantly.

"It's a lime green Victorian on Golden Hill. A guy got killed there this morning, and they think I did it."

"Groovy."

chapter 15

The scene of the crime. The killer always returned there. That's what they said, and they didn't know a barber pole from a fire hydrant, whoever "they" were, Donahoo thought. He never knew one killer who returned to the scene of the crime. Unless they lived there, of course. Then they were stuck. It would look suspicious if they didn't return. But that was the one sole exception that he knew about. Otherwise they stayed away in droves.

Travata looked at 30 0 Ivy.

"It's kinda spooky," she said, but she didn't sound afraid, it was more like she was intrigued, even fascinated. It didn't seem like she had been here before or knew anything more beyond what he had told her. "It's vacant?"

Donahoo said, "Yeah," and passed on what else he wanted to say, that not only was it spooky, he didn't have a ghost of a chance, this was getting dumber by the moment. He got the hot dogs that they'd picked up at the Arco AM/PM on University Avenue off Interstate 805. Oscar Mayer wieners, two for 99¢. He pushed out of her new silver Mercedes 560SL, which she had wanted him to drive, so as to see, later, if the memory seat really worked. It was supposed to return automatically to her configuration. "Let's do it."

There wasn't a yellow tape but there was a cardboard sign pasted to the Victorian's front door. It said, CRIME SCENE. DO NOT ENTER. TRESPASSERS SUBJECT TO ARREST & PROSECUTION.

Donahoo took Travata around the side. He tried a couple of basement windows but they were locked. He got lucky with the window on the back stoop. It was stuck, but eventually gave way. When he got it up, he could reach around to the stoop's back door and open it from the inside. The door to the house itself, in the kitchen, was unlocked.

"Where did it happen?" Travata wanted to know.

Donahoo showed her with a flashlight muted by his capped fingers. He hung on the spot, now cleaned up, where he had found Willie Johnson. The crime lab was fast. It also was good. Saperstein had made it a priority after the FBI flap and O.J. "Right there."

"In the kitchen?"

"Yes." He was watching her, not the spot. "The kitchen is a popular place for murder. Not as popular as the bedroom, mind you, nor the bathroom, but I'd say it ranks third, maybe fourth, after closets."

She shivered. "I'd think basements would be the most popular."

"Not in California. Too much slab construction."

He led the way through the empty dining room and down a narrow hall to the front bedroom with the mattress. He moved the flashlight over it. It was, as he remembered, a Sealy Posturepedic, and pretty plump, it ought to do okay.

"It's a winner," Travata pronounced. He thought she might be a bit nervous but she wasn't showing any signs of being implicated in the frameup. She wasn't making any suspicious moves. "We oughta get some height outa that."

"Oh, we can let it rip, alright," Donahoo agreed. "These Victorians? The high ceilings? They knew what they were doing back then."

"The good old days."

"They were the best."

Travata loosened the chin string on her gaucho hat. She took it off and sailed it into a corner like a Frisbee.

"What are the chances of us getting caught?"

"I dunno. Not much. Maybe one in a hundred?"

"That's good enough for me."

Donahoo unwrapped the hot dogs. He'd put the works on both of them: mustard, ketchup, chopped onions, but he had left the jalapeños off hers, by request. She said she didn't like anything too hot.

"You wanta eat those first?"

"No, during." He was getting the hang of it. He wished Saperstein was there. Show him something about life in the fast lane. "You can handle it, can't you?"

"Hell, yes. Take me out to the ball game."

Donahoo, entranced, watched her undress by the faint light from the tavern across the street, Bertie's. The white blouse fell away like a veil. She wasn't wearing a bra. The long skirt dropped. No panties.

"Coming?"

Yeah, if he didn't watch himself, Donahoo thought. From the neck down, she was breathtaking, awesome. No Irish elf. All Greek goddess. The only flaw was the slightly shortened leg, which she disguised, artfully, by lifting it slightly, like a hunting dog pointing. He gave her the hot dogs to hold.

"You staying in the boots?"

"You got a problem with 'em?"

"Just don't step on me."

Donahoo got undressed. He thought about leaving his shoes on, but they were brogans, size twelve, half-inch soles, and he wasn't the smoothest guy on his feet. He couldn't dance. He shuffled around. Cominsky was always the one with the lessons.

Travata got a miniature boom box tape deck out of her saddle bag. She turned it on. The empty bedroom started to fill with the faint slow music of Ravel's 'Bolero.'

He joined her on the mattress. She gave him his hot dog. They started jumping, baby jumps, slow, in time to the music. They started eating and kissing.

"You're a natural, Tommy," she whispered, pleased.

He had to admit, "I do think I was just waiting to be discovered."

'Bolero' surged on. Louder, faster. They jumped higher, quicker. They connected, linked, attached, became one. 'Bolero' soared. They ate their hot dogs, jumping ever higher. They lost themselves in wild abandon. They timed it perfectly, achieving precisely at the piece's shattering conclusion. They collapsed spent and happy.

"That was my all-time best, Tommy," Travata gasped, holding Donahoo's hand. "I can't think of when I've had a better time."

Donahoo had to agree. It felt like they had knocked the stuffing out of the mattress. Absently, he trailed his fingers along the side and found a rip. There was shredded paper sticking out. He got the flashlight. It wasn't paper.

It was money.

"What is it?"

Donahoo held the flashlight close under his cupped fingers.

"It's a hundred-dollar bill!"

Donahoo looked closer. Yes, it was, a hundred-dollar bill, and there were a lot more of them in the mattress.

"What's it doing there?"

Exactly, Donahoo thought. He thought that he could handle this in one of two ways. He could call Lewis. Or he could walk in front of a bus.

He poked around some more.

"What are you looking for?"

"A bus schedule," he said grimly.

chapter 16

Lewis was ballistic. He stomped around the Victorian, so angry he could hardly speak. He appealed to the heavens. He considered punching a wall. Donahoo felt like he had encountered Hitler on a bad hair day. It was best to let the tirade run its course.

Lewis had them separated. Donahoo sat in a corner of the living room, Travata in a corner of the dining room, so they couldn't communicate without Lewis hearing.

"You, Tommy," Lewis kept saying, and then he would stop, he couldn't get the rest out. Twice he had to go outside and get some air. He would stand there breathing. Deep gulps. Then he'd come back in and start all over. "You, Tommy . . ."

Donahoo and Travata could communicate on these occasions but by this time they didn't have much more to say than Lewis. They had talked it over while waiting and they had decided that the best thing to do was just tell the truth, within reason. Not volunteer anything, but answer questions, adequately if not fully. It had worked pretty well so far. Nobody had asked any questions.

Lewis had come in and taken one look. Travata, the mattress, the money. He had motioned to Vickers and Dugan, a gesture that said, don't speak, just pick it up. Donahoo was surprised about Lewis taking it so hard. He had expected hard, but not *this* hard.

Vickers came in from the front bedroom with a green trash bag. It was filled with money from the mattress.

"There's two of 'em," Vickers said. "Dugan's got the other."

"How much do you think?" Donahoo asked.

Vickers shrugged. "I dunno. Hundreds of thousands?"

Dugan struggled in. "I'd say a million. Gut feeling."

"Fuck," Lewis said. He was getting himself under control. He got his shirt back in his pants. "Call Brinks. Get 'em over here with an armored truck. Vickers, you stand guard out front. Dugan, you take the back." He said, "Dugan, leave the money here."

Donahoo thought, here it comes.

"You, Tommy," Lewis said, and then he changed his mind; he still couldn't do it. He went instead to Travata. He said, "You wanta tell me what happened?"

She said, "You're supposed to ask questions."

He said, "That *was* a question."

"Hey, hey," Donahoo complained. He pushed up from the floor. It was plain that he had to take over. "I can tell you everything you need to know, Lewis. I brought Travata here as part of my investigation . . ."

Lewis whirled. "This isn't your case! It's assigned to Vickers and Dugan!"

"The murder, sure," Donahoo said easily. "But I was investigating Willie Johnson before he got killed, that's the part I'm talking about. The pre-homicide and pre-Vickers pre-Dugan part."

Lewis stared.

"Hey," Donahoo said, taking advantage. "Nobody pulled me off that part. I haven't been charged with anything. I'm still on duty. Hell, you wanta get technical? I've got an *obligation*, Lewis. Next question."

Lewis was still staring. It looked like he might have to go outside again.

"Miss Travata?" Donahoo said. "She's here as a possible material witness. There was a possibility that she had seen this house before, and if she had, it would have a bearing on the case, pre-homicide."

Lewis gave up. "And the mattress?"

"Being human we got carried away."

"Yes, I can see why," Lewis said, looking at Travata. She had her gaucho hat on backwards and looked adorable. Or maybe she had it on sideways. Donahoo wasn't sure. Lewis said, "Uh, what about the uh, problems we talked about?"

"I'm not daffy," Travata told him. "Nor is my father dangerous. He's just a blowhard. He wouldn't harm a cow. He's been yelling at me for years and nothing has ever happened." She thought about which part of her body she ought to show him. Settled for a thigh. "Not a mark."

"Yeah," Donahoo said. "You don't have to worry. We're covered by the trust fund. You don't believe me? Call Herzog, Garfield and Philpott. Ask to talk to Philpott."

"What about Saperstein?"

"I hate to think."

Lewis mulled it over for a while. He was a mess. He'd been disturbed after retiring for the night and he had dressed in a hurry, pulling his clothes on over his pajamas, not because this was an emergency that warranted it, but because he'd been anxious to wring Donahoo's neck. When he stuffed his shirt in his pants, he'd stuffed his pajamas too. It was a double stuff. He was doing it again now. He said, "Tommy, forget lawyer, forget priest. Go straight to the Pope."

chapter 17

Travata dropped Donahoo off at Vic's By the Beach. They kissed good-bye and he watched her drive away in her shiny Mercedes 560SL. This was the first time he had ever dated a rich woman. He thought he might be in love.

It wasn't the money though. It was the advantage it gave her. She could do, more or less, what she pleased. That could get her in a whole lot of trouble. Or it could bring her a lot of joy and happiness. It all depended on her, what kind of person she was. Donahoo had suspected at first that she might have eaten too many macadamia nuts. But now, he thought she just liked a good time. Nothing wrong with that.

He smelled the sea. It was only a couple of blocks away, and it smelled pretty good. He'd grown up nearby, in Solana Beach, and it always called him back, not Solana, but the sea. He wasn't a sailor but he liked to look at it. Or maybe he just liked to smell it.

He went inside and shook hands with two of the three Vics. He had an Old Crow and pocketed some bread sticks. He was feeling good. He had pretty much disposed of Havershot as a suspect. There wasn't enough at stake. Travata's inheritance kicked in five years hence. He couldn't stop it. So why bump off suitors?

No, Donahoo thought. Travata was right. The guy was a blowhard. One of those goddamn control freaks. His time at the helm was running out, and there was nothing he could do about it but stomp his foot and scream, and that's what he was doing. That and waving a gun and making phone calls to Saperstein, but so what?

Forget Havershot. Donahoo thought he had to focus here. He had to think Molino. He tried and he did. In his mind, Mad Marvin Molino was on hold, waiting, as he must, for the plot to thicken, so that he, Donahoo, could be knocked off at the right time. It was a respite, and he could use it to his good advantage, Donahoo thought. He had a fighting chance.

Truthfully, there wasn't a better detective than him around, not around here anyway. That was certain. He had the press clippings to prove it. He'd solved the Purple Admiral Murder Case, the Stardust Donut Shoppe Murder Case, and the Babes in the Woods Murder Case. He'd put out The Balboa Firefly, and he'd stopped Manila Time. He'd even seen to Juarez Justice. He was good.

He had another Old Crow and hid some more bread sticks. Oscar was gonna love him. Yeah, he thought. Detective work. That's what it was going to take, pure and simple. He had panicked there for a moment, the death threats and all, Mad Marvin calling him a potato, Havershot saying he was a jerk. The thing was, though, he was within his rights, and goddamn, that had to count for something. With Mad Marvin, he was doing his sworn duty. Travata, something called there too. Not duty, maybe. But the mating call. Just as strong. Stronger. Donahoo had it all sorted out when he left Vic's By the Beach. He had a week's supply of bread sticks and he was his own man again. He wasn't going to take any more crap from Saperstein. He started across the street for the Toronado.

It blew apart. *Kaboom!*—and it was in flaming pieces.

Donahoo stood looking at the debris. He wondered if it was meant to be a warning or if somebody's timing was off, and it was actually meant to be his coffin.

chapter 18

Saperstein was in police chief heaven. He had never presided over such a feast. He had it all. He had a car bomb and Mad Marvin and Miss Pussy-in-the-Sky and the mattress and the million dollars and Prescott Havershot III. He had Donahoo disobeying a direct order (his). He had Donahoo violating a crime scene (the lime green Victorian). He had Donahoo by the balls.

"Oh, Tommy, this is fulsome," Saperstein said. "I hardly know where to start." He looked at Donahoo for a while. His suspenders almost popped as he lunged across his desk. He started with Travata. "What is wrong with you? You got a sandwich in your ear? I told you—Lewis, you were here, did I tell him?—I told you to stay away from her. I told you she was trouble. Told you she was mental. Told you about the lift. You didn't hear that?"

"Yeah, well," Donahoo said. "A guy's bound to chafe under that kind of restriction, Chief. What I figure, you know, I'm an adult, I oughta be able to date who I want." He was getting uncomfortable, everybody listening, Lewis and all of Squad 5, Vickers and Dugan. They were all crowded into Saperstein's office for this object lesson in humiliation. "If I get home by eleven."

Saperstein's withering glare darkened. "You want a curfew, smartie pants? I can fix it so you don't get supper. No TV."

Lewis said softly, "Chief."

"Okay, maybe Bugs Bunny," Saperstein said. "Daffy Duck." He turned back to Donahoo. "It's the money then, Tommy?" he demanded. "Is that what it is? The money? What is she worth? Fifty million? A hundred? Is that what you're throwing your life and career away for? The money?"

Donahoo didn't answer. It wasn't the money. It was the sex. But he didn't want to tell Saperstein that.

"It's the sex then? This jumping she does? Okay, fine, I understand, but why can't you do it with a poor woman? There's other women, Tommy: waitresses, secretaries, bank tellers. There's plenty of women who would jump at the chance."

Donahoo slumped down in his chair. This was going to be awful, he thought. It was going to go on and on. It would never end.

"Let's talk about the car bomb," Saperstein said. "Somebody wants to kill you? Why is that? Forget I asked. *I* want to kill you. Let's talk about the mattress. Who—tell me, Lewis, help me here?—who ever found a million dollars this way? Down through the ages. Anyone? I didn't think so. Tommy is unique. Very special."

Lewis said softly, "Chief."

"Okay," Saperstein said, relenting. "The Roadrunner. But that's all. I catch you watching Oprah? You ain't no friend of mine."

Donahoo slumped lower.

"Gawd, let him up, willya?" Cominsky begged. His eyes were wet.

"Arrrgh," Saperstein said. "Maybe you're right. What's the use? What's the difference? It's too late anyway." He leaned back, the anger leaving him, like the blood from his face. He looked at Donahoo. "Your car? Blown to ratshit? You know what that means?"

Donahoo couldn't get any lower. "I can't drive it anymore?"

"It means you're a marked man, cutesie," Saperstein said. "You're dead. You're finished, kaput, through. You're over." He said, "You're history, and you oughta be in pictures."

Lewis translated. "We want you to make that video where you testify as to what happened when Mad Marvin popped the Jehovah."

Saperstein added, "So it doesn't matter if you're not around, we can still nail him."

Sure, Donahoo thought. He got it. He wasn't sure he wanted it though. He was still a bit shaken up, having the Toronado blow up in his face, and he didn't want to make a video deposition until he was sure of all the ramifications. He thought there were a couple ways of looking at it. One, Mad Marvin would lay off, thinking the damage was done. Two, Mad Marvin would order a hit, as revenge. He was leaning toward two. Mad Marvin was mad.

Donahoo said, "Uh, I'd like legal counsel, Chief."

Saperstein said, "The camera is set up in the detective parade room."

"Well, I'm making a formal protest," Donahoo told him.

Saperstein said, "You don't need to be formal with me, Tommy."

chapter 19

It was a circus. They were all giving him advice.

Gomez said, "Maybe you better shave again? Remember why Nixon lost to Kennedy."

Palmer said, "Wear a blue shirt and powder your nose."

Cominsky said, "Sarge, don't be nervous, all you gotta do is tell the truth."

Donahoo looked around the detective parade room. He was waiting for someone to advise him to call the whole thing off. He looked to Lewis. Nothing. The crock, Donahoo thought. Lewis knew this was wrong. Maybe a cop had to testify, but if he wanted to wait for the trial, that was his right, right? Nothing. Lewis wouldn't look at him.

They were ready to roll. It was going to be a little fancier than a simple deposition. Davis, the DA, wanted to cover all the bases, seeing how the case was against Mad Marvin. Paul Horncliff, a deputy prosecutor, was going to ask prosecution questions, and Gladys Murd, an attorney from the Public Defender's, was going to ask defense questions, so it wouldn't seem too one-sided. She had volunteered to get some practice. She was new to the office and to law.

"Okay," Horncliff said, moving into the spotlight, "as I understand it, we want to be as detailed and complete as possible here, and Detective Donahoo here . . ."

Donahoo said, "Detective *Sergeant* Donahoo here. Tommy."

"Yes," Horncliff said. "Sergeant. Tommy. Let's get started. We'll swear you in."

Donahoo put his hand on the Bible. Montrose, as a peace officer, administered the oath. Donahoo swore to tell the truth.

Horncliff decided that they'd better have that on video. He asked that the camera start rolling. Donahoo again swore to tell the truth.

Saperstein said, "Can we get on with it?"

Horncliff said, "With all due respect, I must ask you to remain quiet, Chief."

Saperstein said, "You can edit me out, asshole."

Gladys Murd said, "We're not editing out anything. There'll be no cuts."

"Wait a minute," Horncliff said. "You're only here as a courtesy, Gladys. To lend credibility. We don't really need you. Detective Sergeant Tommy can make a statement without cross-examination."

"Wrong," Gladys told him. "You invited me. You're stuck with me."

Horncliff said, "Jesus Christ, you're not here in an official capacity, Gladys."

Gladys said, "That's what you think, counselor. I've talked to Mad Marvin. He's hired me. I'm his lawyer."

"He hired *you?*"

"Check it out."

"Shit, cut," Horncliff said.

Gladys said, "Fuck you, we're rolling."

Donahoo told it exactly the way it happened. He had stopped outside Mad Marvin's estate at Windansea. The Tercel had shown up with the Jehovah's Witnesses. Nobody had responded to their repeated ringing of the bell. The male Witness had climbed over the wall. He, Donahoo, had rushed to the gate, intending to intercede, but he was too late. Mad Marvin, enraged, shot and killed the Witness, no warning. Direct quote: "Who ya fucking with, fishbait?"

Gladys Murd began her questioning.

"Remember, officer, you're under oath," she said. "Now, would you mind telling the court what you were doing outside Mr. Molino's estate the morning in question?"

Donahoo said, "I was parked."

Gladys said, "Yes, but *why* were you parked?"

Saperstein moved closer. Donahoo looked at him. He was sworn to tell the truth. He didn't see how he could do otherwise.

"Well," Donahoo said. "Police Chief Walter Saperstein had told me that Mr. Molino was under investigation by the Bureau of Alcohol, Tobacco and Firearms, and I was attempting to prove him a lying sack of shit."

Horncliff yelled, "Objection!"

Gladys, carried away, shouted, "Overruled!!"

Saperstein said, "You don't want to make this tape, do you, Tommy?"

Donahoo said, "Not with a gun at my head."

Saperstein took the tape out of the camera. He put it in his pocket.

Gladys Murd said, "You can't do that."

Saperstein told her, "Miss Murd, you've got a lot to learn about the law."

Lewis got one of the chairs. He moved it back where it belonged.

"Am I suspended?" Donahoo asked.

"No," Saperstein told him. "I want you out there, Tommy." His smile was a knife. "I want you on the firing line."

chapter 20

Lewis was lugging a green garbage sack when he caught up to Donahoo in the SDPD parking lot. Donahoo thought maybe it was some money from the mattress. Maybe they were trying to buy him off? Of course it could be some stuff for Cominsky's compost. The final degradation.

"It's okay, you don't have to apologize, Lewis," Donahoo said, trying to be positive. "I know why you didn't stand up for me back there. You serve at the bastard's pleasure." He found the key to the van. "He's got you on a string. He holds the scissors. Snip, you're gone, it's back to the Missus. You wouldn't last a month, Lewis. It would be a death sentence. I wouldn't want that kind of thing on my conscience. Would you?"

Lewis changed hands with the trash bag. He hitched up his pants. "Try me. I wouldn't mind."

"Aw," Donahoo said. He didn't know why he was taking it out on Lewis. Saperstein was the guy. "I'm sorry." He glanced back at the police station—to the black hole that was Saperstein's top floor office. "That motherfucker. He's insensitive."

"Hey," Lewis told him. "You got it all wrong. Don't you see?

Saperstein loves you like a son. But he's gotta maintain discipline. You start fucking up, he's gotta give you shit. He can't have anybody thinking they can get away with anything. It would be anarchy."

Donahoo almost laughed. Did they really expect him to swallow that?

"Just to show you." Lewis opened the sack and took out a big bulletproof vest. "The chief ordered this for you. See here, it's your size. XLT. Extra large, tall."

Donahoo took it. He'd been thinking of getting one himself. He took off his jacket and tried it on. It was heavy but he felt safe in it.

"I got this for you myself," Lewis said. "If it's Prescott Havershot III, not Mad Marvin, who is gunning for you, you oughta be wearing this sucker." He took a metal jockstrap out of the bag. "I got it in a leather shop. See here, it's your size. XLL. Extra large, long."

"Now goddamn," Donahoo complained, "you can't flatter me, Lewis. I'm not making that video, and that's final."

"Nobody wants you to," Lewis said soothingly. "That's water under the bridge. Cowshit in the meadow. We're looking ahead now. What's best for you. We all love you, Tommy." He pressed the jockstrap on Donahoo. "We want you in the Witness Protection Program."

Donahoo stared at him dumbly. "What?"

"Think about it. You qualify. Sole witness. FBI-related case. We can't make it without you. And, not only have you been threatened, there's been an attempt against your life."

"A warning."

"Don't quibble."

Donahoo thought that he wasn't. Whoever destroyed the Toronado, they could have fixed it so he went with it, not when he was walking toward it, just far enough away to escape injury.

"No, I don't think so, Lewis," he said. "I still figure I've got a shot here. Mad Marvin's not going to hit me till I'm discredited by the Willie Johnson case. *If* I don't make a video. So there's still time to outfox him. *If* I'm on the job. I'm no help to myself hiding in the hills somewhere."

"Yeah, but you don't know it was Mad Marvin who waxed your car, Tommy," Lewis said. "It could have been Prescott Havershot III. He's just as pissed at you as Mad Marvin. Maybe more."

Donahoo again didn't think so. He was inclined to side with Travata. The guy was all bark. Mostly, anyway.

"You heard Travata," Donahoo said. "There's no reason for her to lie. You saw yourself how she likes me."

Lewis sighed. "Women. You see what's happening? You're blinded by love."

"I'm not in love."

"No, but you're thinking about it. That's just as bad. You're just as blind."

"Wrong again."

"Tommy. Be honest with yourself, willya? For a minute, delete Travata, she doesn't exist. Pretend Havershot is giving you a hard time for some other reason. A bad debt or whatever. He's making threats and waving a gun in your face. You think you'd kiss it off and walk away? Bullshit. You'd take it seriously. You'd be so far up his ass you'd need a medical degree. There's only one reason you're not. A woman."

"Yeah," Donahoo said, unlocking the van. "And I haven't had one for a while, okay?" He was starting to feel sorry for himself. "I haven't had one I could keep for . . ." He stopped, suddenly overcome by the memories, the loss. He turned back to Lewis. "I'm not making the video. I'm not giving Travata up. Thanks for the jockstrap. Goodbye."

"Nobody's asking you to give her up. It's just until Mad Marvin's trial. How long is that gonna be? Six months? A year?"

"No."

"Tommy. You gotta get with the program. It's the only way to stay alive."

"No."

"Tommy. Do it for us. We all love you."

Donahoo almost had the key in the van's ignition. Something made him pull it away. He offered it to Lewis.

"You love me? Start the van, Lewis. But wait until I get behind something."

Lewis looked at him. He rolled up his trash bag. He turned around and walked away. Donahoo watched him go. Yeah, he thought. He knew all about love. He'd been loved before.

chapter 21

Public Library. Main Branch. California Room. Donahoo had a lot of other things to check out. Who had blown up the Toronado and why, was it just a warning, or a bungled hit? Who had killed Willie Johnson to frame him, and why hadn't they returned for the million dollars in the mattress, unless, of course, they didn't know about the money, and that seemed to be the case. How to stay out of the Witness Protection Program? He didn't trust the FBI. Etcetera, etcetera. But he had put off this particular task long enough.

Lewis, the crock, he was right, Donahoo thought. He had to admit it. He had been blinded by love, again. If not love, incipient love. Nascent. Germinal. Maybe it wasn't here but it was coming. He had to look up the Havershots. He'd have done it sooner, it would have been prudent, it would have been wise, but, he was being honest here, he had been afraid of what he might find, especially as to Travata.

It was still hard to do though. He felt kind of unmanly and sneaky. This wasn't something he would normally do and certainly nothing he had done before. Most women, any he'd known, you couldn't look them up in the library. You were lucky you could look them up in the phone book. He was setting a precedent. Breaking new ground.

The clerk gave him a fat file. It was about the size of a whoopee cushion. He took it over to a desk and opened it up.

First clipping. PRESCOTT HAVERSHOT HANGED FOR MURDER. FINIS WRIT TO SORDID LOVE TRIANGLE. Donahoo picked it off the pile. The date was March 12, 1880. There was a photo of Prescott, another of his victim, Lucas Walker, and a third of Prescott's wife, Annie. They were pictured in fancy oval frames.

Donahoo read the story. Prescott, founder of Coronado Shores, had caught Lucas, his construction foreman, consorting with Annie. The reporter stated it delicately. 'Lucas and Annie were joined together. They were jumping up and down on Prescott's bed.'

Oh, migod, Donahoo thought. It was a family tradition. And it went back more than a hundred years!

He picked through a few more clippings. The Coronado Shores land development company had collapsed. Annie Havershot had died, destitute, shunned, in an El Cajon poorhouse. Prescott Havershot, Jr., the only issue, was raised in a Catholic orphanage.

Whoa. Donahoo wasn't sure he wanted to know any more. This was awful. The family was star-crossed.

He took a deep breath and got another clipping. Years had passed. Junior was a man now. Prescott Havershot II. He'd made it big in railways and on the stock market. The start of the family's fabulous fortune.

There was a photo. A cocky guy in a cocked hat. He looked like he owned the world.

Donahoo took a close look. It belatedly struck him that this was Travata's grandfather. This was the guy who had set up the overly protective trust.

There was no stopping now. He had to dig deeper. Maybe he would find out why. He picked through some more clippings.

Nothing of particular interest. Then a big story about Prescott Havershot II marrying San Diego socialite Mary Astor Bollinger-Boogle.

Donahoo looked at the wedding photo. Travata was the absolute image of her grandmother Mary. It was all there. The big green eyes. The overly generous mouth. The bank robber's nose.

The wedding was a major social event. Two full pages of photos in a rotogravure section. The wedding guests were having fun, drinking, dancing, playing games. Pinning the tail on the donkey. Spinning the bottle. Here was one of the bride and groom. Jumping on a trampoline. Looking expectant. They couldn't wait to get off.

Yeah, that's what it was, a family tradition, Donahoo thought. It must have been handed down.

He went through the rest of the file. It was mostly all Wall Street stuff. The Havershot empire expanding like cancer cells. Acquisitions, takeovers, mergers. Communications, transportation, oil, gas, and, finally, American Steel. Prescott Havershot II seamlessly metamorphosing into Prescott Havershot III.

There had been a period when the Havershots were not especially newsworthy. When media attention resumed, the focus was on III, not II. The focus was on Travata. Debutante ball. Junior League. Active in several high profile charities. Nothing about her accident.

Here was something though. Erskine Fotheringham, engaged to marry Travata Havershot, crashed his Morgan sports car into the Havershot circular driveway fountain, suffering a back injury. Fotheringham was alone at the time. The police said he was drunk but no charges were laid. Shortly thereafter he disappeared.

Disappeared? Donahoo read that again. No mistake. The guy had disappeared.

Disappeared. Donahoo couldn't get the word out of his head. It could be innocent enough—maybe Fotheringham was embarrassed? His family sent him to Europe?—but it also could be a sinister foreshadowing.

Under the circumstances, and there were a lot of circumstances, it could go either way, Donahoo thought. It was something to think about, and, eventually, ask about, but he didn't want to ask right now.

Right now he didn't think he could stand it if he found out something bad about Travata. He'd have to wait until he got his courage up. There was too much going on and he was feeling the pressure. Saperstein pissing on him. Lewis pushing Witness Protection. The bulletproof vest. The steel jockstrap. Well, the vest anyway. He still hadn't put on the jockstrap.

He looked around carefully. There were about six bums at the various tables in the California Room. Any one of them could have been hired by Prescott Havershot III. Paid to make him disappear. Or worse.

Donahoo hurried to the restroom and put on the jockstrap.

chapter 22

El Cajon Boulevard. Texas Street. Donahoo had been driving aimlessly, or so he thought, but now he was looking for Clancy Holden, trying to pick her out from the other girls on the street. They were all dressed much the same. Big unzipped jackets. Short tight skirts. She'd be the bitty one.

He moved up to Oregon, to Folsom's Tennis, found a parking spot, watched for her, she could pop up anywhere. Fairly soon she came out of the San Diego Chicken Pie Shop. She had a coffee in a cardboard cup.

He called, "Hey, Pretty Woman!"

She grinned and walked over. "You looking for a good time, Charlie?"

Donahoo thought that he sure wouldn't mind. Clancy was her dazzling self in handlebar braids and precious little titties nestled like Easter eggs in her half-zipped jacket. He pushed open the van's passenger side door and she slipped in beside him. Her lips glistened and she smelled like lemons.

"How would you like it?" Clancy asked. "I'm quoting preferred rates here. Twenty dollars for a Pooner Nooner. Fifty for the Fabulous

Fantasy Five. A hundred for the Midnight Deluxe Special."

Donahoo took a sip of her coffee. He said, "Vickers and Dugan. A couple of Homicide cops. Have you talked to them?"

She nodded and looked away. "They talked to me. Wanted to know if I'd given you an address for Willie Johnson." She turned back to him. "I said no."

"What did they say?"

" 'Thank you.' "

"Did they look surprised?"

"No."

"How did they look?"

"Like they had your ass."

Yeah, Donahoo thought. They had him for two hundred dollars of petty cash. He thought that he'd rather go down for sexual harassment than for stealing two hundred dollars.

"Uh, I'm in a spot here, Clancy," Donahoo confessed. "I don't want you to change your story or anything. I know how religious you are and that your word is your bond and stuff. But I do wonder if you might reconsider about whether or not you can help me with Willie Johnson."

She got a puzzled expression. "You still looking for him? The paper says he's dead, Donahooie."

"Yeah. I know. What it doesn't say, I found him."

"You're the 'unidentified' cop?"

"Uh-huh. That's me."

She considered for a moment. "Okay. So what's the spot?"

"Well," Donahoo said. He decided to tell her everything. If it compromised the investigation, so what? He was running on empty. "I found him maybe sixty seconds after he got bumped. I heard shots and ran inside, and there he was."

She stared at him. "You're not shitting me?"

"No. Then Vickers and Dugan arrived and looked around and found the murder weapon and it turned out to be one of *my* guns. Stolen from my place last week."

"You *are* shitting me."

"No. Then, last night, I went back to the place, and I found a million dollars in Willie's mattress."

"You definitely are shitting me."

"No. A million bucks. Exactly. It's been counted."

"Willie Johnson?"

"I swear to Christ."

"Wow," Clancy said. She fell silent. She looked like she was trying to suspend disbelief. "A million dollars? Willie Johnson?"

Donahoo nodded solemnly.

"This is what they call the smoking gun?"

"It's what I call deep caca. Vickers and Dugan, they're trying their best to pin the murder on me, and if I don't come up with something soon, preferably the real killer, it's possible I will be charged. My gun, my fingerprints, and I had the opportunity. The only thing they're missing is a motive."

"A million dollars is motive."

"Yeah. But I didn't keep it."

"Maybe they thought you gave it back to divert suspicion."

"Yeah. That's possible."

Clancy sipped thoughtfully at her coffee.

"Uh, listen," Donahoo said. "I appreciate how your mind works. But I was hoping, you know, if we could concentrate on the positive, rather than the negative. I was hoping, in view of the circumstances, that you might want to, uh, review, that's the word, review what you told me yesterday about Willie."

"That I didn't know anything about him?"

"Yes."

"Well I just reviewed and I still don't know anything."

Donahoo looked at her. He knew all along she wouldn't tell a lie. He'd been dealing with her since she was in middle school. But he'd been living in hope there was always a first time.

"Damn, that's too bad," he said. "For me." He reached for the ignition key. "My only hope is to track Willie's recent movements in Golden Hill. He came back, that's plain, and he came back for a reason, that's even plainer. So who did he see? Relatives, friends, business associates? Maybe some home boy new outa prison?"

"I dunno."

"Neither do I. Nor do Vickers and Dugan. Not that they're trying very hard."

"Dead-end?"

"Blank wall." Donahoo was going to turn the key. He said, "It's a bitch. All that money."

Clancy finished her coffee. "No use crying over that. It's gone."

"Oh, the million, yeah," Donahoo said. He started up the van. "But what I figure, a guy's got a million dollars in his mattress, there's no telling what he's got in the bank. The mattress could be birdshit. Never mind canaries. I oughta be looking for elephants."

Clancy reached over and turned off the motor. "You think there's more?"

"Why not?"

She looked at him. He looked at her. The chemistry started. Oh, oh, he thought. Here we go. He knew what was happening, and he couldn't stop it. They were making one of those unspoken agreements. They had just become partners. She was going to do her best to give him the real killer. He was going to give her first crack at whatever money came with him. They didn't have to say a word. They'd just made that arrangement. He had never done anything remotely like it before, but he was running on empty, and he was running scared.

"I'll ask around," Clancy said. "I'll be in touch." Her hand left the key and moved toward his crotch. He didn't try to stop her. Still, she looked to him for permission. "A Pooner Nooner?"

"Uh," Donahoo said, "tell me what to do. I've resisted before through my strength of devotion to sworn duty. But, alas, I've been abandoned by the department I love, and have served so nobly . . ."

Clancy laughed and gave him a whack. She cried out in pain. The Chinese eyes widened. "Wow," she said admiringly. "You sure pack it in there, Donahooie."

chapter 23

Donahoo went home to celebrate another wasted day. He thought he should stop asking questions. They only raised more questions and more loose ends. He'd never had so many loose ends. He couldn't remember them all. He was going to have to write them down.

He got out his solace, the Old Crow, and the cat version, a bread stick, for Oscar.

He said, "How you doing, guy?" and Oscar went crunch. It really wasn't his cat. It was Monica's cat. Monica had left him two things when she left. She had left him a cat and a saucer. She hadn't even left him a cup.

He had a funny story about the cup. He had been going around complaining he didn't have a cup and there was a young cop hawking, this was at the SDPD, cups made by his grandmother, they were speckled, blue/white, like enamel, only they were ceramic. She put names on them. Bruce was taking orders. He had a list of names. Paul. Nancy. Alex. Rudy. Donahoo said put his name down, TOMMY, and then he thought, this was how he was thinking at the time—he'd been left with nothing, not even a cup—he said, no, don't put his name on it, put MINE. So Bruce wrote down MINE, and Donahoo's cup came back saying, BRUCE.

He got a pen and a notepad. He started making the loose ends list.

The Beretta, for example. He had been wondering about it forever. How did somebody get in the apartment to steal it?

The slider on the balcony was left open, of course, so Oscar could go outside to break wind, but a burglar would need a fire ladder or a grappling hook to reach the balcony. No, it had to be via the front hall entrance, or, if it was a child burglar, the bathroom window.

Donahoo sighed and sipped on his Old Crow. He'd talked to all the neighbors and none of them had seen anybody suspicious. He'd talked to everybody but Vera. He and Vera weren't talking. Vera had taken advantage of him during her husband Cody's chemotherapy.

He wondered if he ought to put on the record, *'I Wonder Who's Kissing Her Now.'* Yesterday, he swore he'd never play it again, not while he could jump to *'Bolero,'* but his visit to the California Room had shaken him. Travata had never mentioned Erskine Fotheringham. She certainly hadn't mentioned his disappearance.

What happened with Vera, who couldn't drive, Donahoo had told her he'd be happy to take Cody to chemotherapy, and also that he'd be available in any emergency. Pretty soon she had him going for Chinese food and pizza, and then Lottery tickets. The Lottery tickets did it. He said, "What's the emergency, Vera?"

And she said, "The store closes in fifteen minutes."

Of course, as soon as Cody died, Vera learned to drive, and now she was purring all over the place in Cody's Buick.

Donahoo poured another Old Crow. He wondered if he should call Travata. Ask her the Fotheringham question. He had to ask her sooner or later. Why put it off?

He picked up the phone and called Vera. He said, "Hi, it's me. Listen, have you seen anybody suspicious around here lately?"

"Yeah, you," she said and hung up.

Donahoo put the phone back. He thought he ought to charge her chemotherapy mileage. He hadn't kept track but he could make up something. Let's see. Twenty-two trips to Kaiser. Six, no seven, miles each way. That's 22 times 14 equals 308 miles times 40 cents equals $123.20. Maybe he oughta charge her a buck a mile?

The phone rang. He picked up. He said, "Vera?"

Cominsky said, "It's me, Sarge. Whatcha doing?"

"Forget it, Cominsky," Donahoo said, "I'm not going into the Witness Protection Program."

chapter 24

What Cominsky had in mind was a poker game. They put it together at Gomez's place in Chula Vista. His wife was visiting relatives
in Mexicali. There were seven of them at the game, counting Gomez.
Donahoo and Cominsky. Palmer and Montrose. Lewis and a friend,
an anal retentive kind of guy named Wilson Pomfret.

"We oughta do this more often," Gomez said. He was winning.
"You're all in? I raise again."

"Gomez, you can't raise on yourself," Palmer said. He was the
expert. "We all met your raise. Now we play. Gimme two cards."

Gomez said, "Before I do, are there any more rules you wanta
make up, Palmer?"

Palmer said, "Yeah, the host can't go away winners."

Gomez looked at him. "Oh, why not?"

"Because you live here."

Donahoo wondered where in the hell Lewis had found Wilson
Pomfret. The guy looked like a pelican, he had the beady fish eyes,
the long nose, the wattle chin. He was wearing a pelican gray suit
and he sat strangely still, the way a pelican, after a few wing flaps,
can sit in the sky.

Gomez started dealing draw cards. Two to Palmer, two to Montrose. Pomfret was still thinking.

"Uh, somebody's gotta help me here," Pomfret pleaded. "Holding three of a kind. What should I do? Draw two cards or one card?"

Palmer said, "Two."

Pomfret said, "Why?"

Palmer told him, "The odds of making four of a kind are 22 to 1. On the other hand, drawing one card, the odds are 46 to 1."

"What about making a full house?"

"The odds are practically the same. They're 15 to 1 versus 14 2/3 to 1."

"So it doesn't matter which?"

"Not much."

Montrose said, "What are the odds of playing this fucking game?"

Lewis said, "I told you. He's learning, okay?"

Pomfret took two cards. Lewis asked for one. Cominsky got three, the limit. Donahoo took two, and Gomez stayed pat.

"Uh, what is it you do, Mr. Pomfret?" Donahoo asked.

Lewis said, "He's in offshore investments."

Pomfret said, "You can call me Wilson, Tommy."

Donahoo said, "Can I call you Will?"

Pomfret said, "I'd rather you didn't."

"Offshore, huh?" Cominsky asked, interested. "Is that legal?"

Lewis gave him a dirty look. Pomfret smiled tightly.

Donahoo couldn't remember Lewis ever bringing anybody to a poker game. He checked his draw cards. He had nothing. A deuce and a four to go with his two kings. He shouldn't have kept the ace kicker. He was playing too conservatively.

"Bets," Gomez demanded.

Donahoo threw in, then he got up and wandered into the kitchen. He had the uncomfortable feeling that they were all watching him. They were worried about him, he knew that, he wouldn't go into the Witness Protection Program, and he appreciated their concern, but it still spooked him. He was sorry he had agreed to come. He'd leave, but he had come with Cominsky, in Cominsky's car, and he didn't want to drag Cominsky away. It would spoil the game. He wondered if he should call a cab. Chula Vista to Uptown. Maybe he should win some money first. He made himself a fresh Old Crow.

Pomfret was saying, "Three and two, that's a full house, right?"

Montrose was saying, "Fuck."

Donahoo got the phone. He dialed Travata's pager number. Left a message. He thought maybe she would come and get him. They'd go jump somewhere and he'd ask her about the disappearance of Erskine Fotheringham. He thought maybe they had a Rumplestiltskin going here. Maybe the guy leaped into the sky and never came down?

Palmer yelled, "Are you in?"

"Yeah."

Donahoo returned to the game with his new Old Crow. It was no-peeky baseball, one-eyed jacks wild. He looked at his down cards. Well, he thought, maybe he'd pass on the cab. Call a yacht.

"Cominsky," Pomfret said. "Lewis tells me you're an inventor. What kind of things do you invent?"

"Oh, I'm working on a few things, alright," Cominsky told him. "There's a couple got a pretty good shot. Water ear plugs and revolving motorcycle helmets."

Donahoo thought, *sure.* But he had to admit that Cominsky's idea for traffic lights on sidewalk ATMs had the makings of a winner. The idea was that you could see the lights a block away or more, green for if the ATM was open, red for if it was closed. So far, no bank would invest in it, but that was management's fault, not the idea's. Apparently management actually wanted ATM customers to find a parking spot, feed a meter, walk a block, discover the ATM closed, and say, *Oh, dear.*

Cominsky had summed it up. "You can beat almost anything, but you can't beat dumb, Sarge."

Donahoo's cards started turning bad. A pair of nines and then zip. He wasn't feeling too good either. It must be all the excitement. He thought maybe he should pass on the yacht. Call an ambulance.

Pomfret showed a card. "This is a one-eyed jack, right?"

The phone rang. Gomez got it. He was in the kitchen getting the sandwiches out of the fridge.

"Tommy?" he said. "It's for you. It's a lady."

Donahoo took it on the extension in the den. Gomez was waiting to hear the pickup. There was a click as he hung up.

"Hello?" Donahoo said. He was pretty sure it was Travata but there was a wild chance it was Vera. He didn't want to take that chance. "Who's this?"

Travata laughed. She said, "How many ladies you got returning calls this time of night?"

He said, "It's my ad in the PhoneMates. They just won't leave me alone. I guess I shouldn't of been so honest."

"In describing yourself?"

"In saying what I wanted."

She laughed again. He thought that was one of the special things about her. She could laugh at anything. It must be the brain damage.

"I thought we were going to give it a rest," she said, "for a night." There was a pause. "Tell me you changed your mind."

"I changed my mind."

"Good. Let me finish dinner. I'm with my parents, so I don't know when that's gonna be. Can I call you back?"

"Sure. When do think?"

"Pretty soon."

Donahoo was going to wait. He had planned to wait. He couldn't. He took a drink of Old Crow.

"Uh," he said, "Erskine Fotheringham, your fiancé who disappeared. What's the story on that?"

"Erskine?"

"Yeah."

There was a long pause. Montrose called from the dining room. "Are you in or out?"

Donahoo lowered the phone and covered the mouthpiece. "In!"

Travata was talking when he got back on the line. She was saying, ". . . I guess that's what comes from dating a detective. We've gotta talk about this now?"

"Why not?"

"Okay," she said. "I plead guilty. He injured his back in a car accident and after that we could only have sex in one position. He had to be on his back. The doctor said it was a permanent condition.

That wasn't satisfactory to me. So I told him to disappear. He did."

Donahoo said, "Yeah, well, I'm glad we got that straightened out."

Travata said, "Me, too. I'll call you."

Donahoo returned to the table. They were already looking at their hands. He picked up his cards, found four diamonds, short a jack for a royal flush, short a jack for cab money.

The betting was heavy. Three times around. Everybody stayed in.

"Okay, two," Montrose said. "Be kind."

Donahoo watched the other draws with increasing satisfaction. They might have stayed in, but they were on the come. They all looked desperate. He finished his Old Crow. Everybody had their cards. Donahoo still hadn't looked at his. He was starting to feel real punk.

"Uh, where are you offshore, Wilson?" he asked, and Pomfret said, "The New Hebrides."

Montrose started the betting. Gomez folded. Left the table.

Donahoo said, "How did you get into that, Wilson?"

Pomfret said, "Oh, I just sort of drifted."

The phone rang. Donahoo finally got to look at his draw card. Jack of diamonds.

Someone, it sounded like Gomez, asked, "Is there a Tommy here?"

Someone else yelled, "Donahoo? No, he went home. He left with that black hooker."

Donahoo found Pomfret the pelican looking at his hand. Pomfret said, smiling, "I guess that beats my two pair."

Oooooh. Donahoo felt himself going. The lights were getting fuzzy. The room was starting to rotate.

"You've played this game before, haven't you, Wilson?" Donahoo said, and he passed out.

chapter 25

Interstate 8. In the Sand Hills. Still California but approaching Arizona. Six o'clock in the morning. Only faint light on account of low cloud cover. An old Chevy station wagon screaming.

Donahoo woke up in the back seat. Wilson Pomfret tossed him a big silver thermos.

"Pelican Man," Donahoo said. He twisted the top off the thermos. He felt like his head was coming off with it. "You wouldn't have a tub of aspirin?"

Pomfret laughed and dug around in his jacket. A small bottle came flying back. He said, "You're a goddamn horse. You shoulda gone down after the first hand."

Donahoo took the aspirin with the coffee, which was warm, not hot, but still good. He felt for his Colt Python. He didn't have it.

"Let me guess," he said, looking around. The freeway was empty. He didn't know where he was. The station wagon, he saw the insignia, saw it was an old Chevy, big and powerful, doing eighty. "I'm being kidnapped into the Witness Protection Program?"

"Yes and no," Pomfret told him, still amused. He was looking at him in the rearview mirror. "We're just trying to use some psychology here."

Donahoo was more interested in the mechanics. "How did you pull it off? I was guarding my glass like it was my liver. It was never out of my sight."

"We spiked the Old Crow. Switched bottles."

"Everybody in on it?"

"Yeah."

Donahoo was going to ask, Even Cominsky? Then he remembered that Cominsky had taken him to the game.

"We thought we'd get you this far, a clean break, nobody on your tail," Pomfret said. He still wanted to talk psychology. "Home free. *Fait accompli.* Then you could make up your mind. It's a lot easier to go into the program if you're already in it. That's the psychology part."

Donahoo wished he had the Python. It was the only way he knew of stopping a car going eighty miles an hour. Stick the thing in Pomfret's ear. If he started wrestling with the guy, they'd go off the road, roll for sure.

"You know what I'm saying?" Pomfret continued. "All those pressures? How you gonna think straight? Mad Marvin. Willie Johnson. Prescott Havershot and the lovely leaping Travata. Clancy Holden and those handlebars? Saperstein?" He was still looking in the rearview, holding real steady like a pelican. He said, "The danger. The mystery and the intrigue. The bing and the bang."

Donahoo put out a hand. "What have you got for me?"

"A couple things to keep you amused. How about Little Duckie and Teach-Time Fun Hippo?" Pomfret handed back some ID. It said that Wilson Pomfret was a Special Agent of the Federal Bureau of Investigation.

Donahoo gave it back. "What else?"

Pomfret passed over a large manila envelope.

"You're out of the woods. We had seven vehicles leave Gomez's place all at the same time. Two out of the garage and five from that big side yard behind the high fence. Seven vehicles going in seven directions. No way of telling which one you were in. If anybody was watching, they wouldn't know who to follow, and anyway, they didn't follow us. They'd have picked us off by now if they did."

Donahoo was going through the contents of the manila envelope. He had a new driver's license, new car registration, new car insurance, new bank account, new credit cards. He had a new birth certificate and a new Social Security number. He had a new passport. His new name was Donald Myers.

"*Donald* Myers?"

"Actually, *Jersey* Myers," Pomfret said. "Everybody calls you Jersey. That's where you're from. You see your birth certificate? Trenton, New Jersey. That's how you got the name."

"Jersey?"

"Yeah."

Donahoo looked again at his passport photo. It was almost, but not quite, as bad as his driver's license photo, which was for Illinois, not California. He didn't look like himself either. He had very short white hair and a big black bushy mustache to go with his big black bushy eyebrows. He looked very tough. He looked mean.

"Uh, Wilson," he said. "Jersey Myers. That sounds like a wiseguy. It doesn't sound like an architect."

"No."

"Let me rephrase. It doesn't sound like an architect."

"So?"

"So if I'm going into a protection program, and I'm not saying, yet, if I'm going, how come I'm not an architect or something? How come I'm a wiseguy?"

"Simple. You don't know anything about being an architect, Jersey. Or, for that matter, pick a profession. Tinker? Tailor? What you know is being a cop, and you can't go into hiding as a cop. What you know second best is a crook. You deal with them all the time. You can go into hiding as a crook."

"Why can't I go into hiding as a cop?"

"Please. Too obvious. And cops deal with crooks. So pretty soon a crook is gonna recognize you."

"In some new city?"

"Anywhere. Mad Marvin wants your head? There are gonna be circulars out there."

"Circulars?"

"With your picture on 'em."

Donahoo put his new credentials aside. He hadn't thought of that. Wanted posters, wanted dead, not alive, being circulated around The Mob, being handed to hundreds of ambitious shooters, wanting to get on the good side of Mad Marvin.

"Well," Pomfret said. He wasn't looking in the rearview anymore. He was paying attention to his driving now. "Jersey. Have you made up your mind?"

Donahoo thought for a while. He was thinking of all the people he was going to miss. Gomez and Montrose. Palmer, Cominsky, Lewis. Gawd, when he thought about it, he might even miss Saperstein. But mostly he was thinking about how to get Travata into the Witness Protection Program. He didn't want to be crooked and alone. It sounded depressing. "Do I get to have a significant other?"

"You want Oscar? That's nice."

"I was thinking of Miss Havershot."

Pomfret shook his head. "I wouldn't advise it. She could be part of the problem."

"No." Donahoo couldn't accept that. He saw Travata as separate, estranged, completely apart from Havershot. Maybe it was Havershot, not Mad Marvin, who ordered the car bombing, but Travata, he knew this in his heart, had no knowledge of it. He didn't have many gut feelings but he had that one. He said, "You're wrong."

"And you're not thinking clearly, Jersey. Havershot has incredible resources. If Travata were to disappear, he could bring them to bear, spare no expense. He could locate her and find you. I know how good it's been for you with the girl. But you really ought to keep your feet on the ground."

Oh, yeah? Donahoo was going to argue but he realized it was useless. Pomfret was right. If he went into the program, he'd have to go alone, at least initially. That would only be fair to Travata. It had to be tested. To see if it worked. He didn't want to endanger her. He said, "How long do you think this picnic would last?"

"Hard to tell. Till, of course, Mad Marvin is convicted, sent away. Then it depends. He might be madder at you than he is now. On the other hand, he might listen to reason, realize he isn't going to get any time off, good behavior, if something happens to you. So what I think is I don't know."

"So you'd want me to come back to testify?"

"Yes."

"And then sneak back into hiding?"

"Well, that's more what you'd wanta do."

Donahoo dug deeper into the manila envelope. There were several wads of cash, used twenties. He figured maybe two thousand dollars. Tight rein. He'd have to behave if he wanted more. "I get an allowance?"

"Until you get a job."

"As a crook?"

"You'll find something."

"What? Robbing convenience stores?"

Pomfret sighed. "Now, now. Don't be difficult, Jersey. I've been doing this for thirty years. Never had a witness who couldn't get a job. What happens, usually, something will come up in the government. Social Security clerk, maybe. Or a postman is good."

"Delivering mail?"

"Lots of fresh air and exercise. Ever take a good look at the legs on a postman? That's why they wear them short pants."

Donahoo counted the money. Yes, two thousand. Plus, he checked the registration, clear title to the station wagon. "Is there a limit on the credit cards?"

"You betchum. Five hundred each. I want you paying in, not taking out. I want you building your credit rating in your new identity."

Donahoo thought that he was broke. Two thousand dollars and a lousy station wagon. A five-hundred limit on his credit cards. It didn't seem hardly enough. He wondered if he could get the pot sweetened. Maybe they'd pay his rent or something. Or, what the hell, if he had to go into hiding, maybe they would pay his way somewhere nice, maybe to Hawaii, or even Tahiti. He could go to Kuala Lampur, maybe. Learn a new language. "What are the chances of a foreign posting?"

"Canada I wouldn't recommend anymore," Pomfret said. "Vancouver, it's getting too big, too crowded, too expensive. Everywhere you go there's a line a mile long, and when you get to the end there's a Chinaman at the cash register. Calgary, they've got that stampede, it draws a big crowd, people from all over, somebody could see you. The prairies are better. They've got places so remote they don't even show 'em on TV. Winnipeg, Moose Jaw, Saskatoon. But you'd freeze your nuts off. It's worse than Iceland. Toronto, you don't want to go to Toronto, too many Italians. Montreal, too many frogs. But for a guy who wants to stay on the move, back and forth, in and out, it's workable. I had a guy once, he was Nick in New York, Frenchie in Montreal."

"How about other countries?"

"You don't wanta go abroad. It'll get you every time. Mexico, the trots. South America, revolutions. The Philippines, hepatitis. In Singapore they'll get you for chewing gum. The whole Far East is a cesspool. Nice pictures, lousy reality. Hong Kong used to be something. There were things you could do. Get a suit tailored. Have dinner on a junk. Save a little girl some poor family doesn't want before they drown her. But not anymore. The Commies."

"How about Europe?"

"No."

Donahoo wondered what was left. The Middle East? He thought to look at the small print on his driver's license. The word popped up at him. Cairo.

He screamed it. "Cairo?!!"

"Cairo," Pomfret said. He pronounced it correctly, care-oh. "Southern Illinois. An historic little town at the confluence of the Mississippi and Ohio rivers. Of great significance to the North in the Civil War. And, for you, a sensible choice, Jersey."

Donahoo stared, shocked, baffled, at the back of Pomfret's head. Cairo, Illinois. Little Egypt. He vaguely remembered reading or hearing about it. The part he remembered was that it was a fucking pesthole and that it had race riots. He said, "Cairo? Well, now here's a choice for you, Wilson. You can change that, or you can make a U-turn. I'm not going to any fucking Cairo. They've got race riots there."

"Had," Pomfret corrected. "Used to. Not anymore." He glanced in the rearview. "There's even a move afoot to demolish all the fire-gutted buildings."

"Make a U," Donahoo ordered. "Don't wait for the next inter-change. Just bump across the median. I'll pay any fine."

"That's how you feel about it?"

"That's how."

Pomfret slowed and pulled off onto the shoulder. He pushed out of the station wagon but held the door open.

Donahoo, alarmed, said, "Now what are you doing?"

Pomfret said, "Taking a leak."

Donahoo looked for other traffic. "Here?"

"You know, you're an ingrate," Pomfret said, visibly angry. "I set up, on short notice, a new identity for you, to the best of my abil-ity . . ." He was starting to choke up. "The director had to approve overtime . . . in order to save your life." He wiped his nose. "And this is the thanks I get?"

Donahoo said, "Here's a hankie. I'm not going to Cairo."

Pomfret slammed the door. He started away, then turned around, came back. He opened the door. "The race riot you mentioned? It was more a series of continuing events than an actual riot. Every night, whites would arm themselves, get into their cars, and drive around looking for blacks. Blacks would arm themselves, get into their cars, drive around looking for whites. This went on for years and years."

That long? Donahoo wondered why Pomfret would reveal that kind of information. Cairo was sounding worse, not better. He'd have to be an idiot to hide out there.

"So why are you telling me?"

"Why would you think, huh?" Pomfret demanded. "What would be my motive? Well, here's what you want to know—it's the measure of the place! In all that time there were only a couple three killings. Those fuckers can't shoot straight." He slammed the door. He started off again. He turned briefly to shout. "You yellow bastard!" Then he scrambled up a steep sand dune sloping away from the freeway's shoulder.

Donahoo was stunned. He sat dumbly watching. Pomfret reached the top of the dune and plunged over and disappeared.

"Hey," Donahoo said. He got out of the station wagon. Pomfret was gone. This is crazy, Donahoo thought. Nobody would go all the way over the dune just to take a leak. He wondered if Pomfret might be angry enough to ditch him.

It was deathly still. Donahoo felt like the world had stopped. He stood looking at the V at the top of the dune that marked Wilson Pomfret's departure. It was like the sight on a gun. In his imagination, Donahoo aimed, fired. He waited for the nitro to explode. For the V to heave. To hear the shot. He waited and nothing happened. The Sand Hills were silent.

Well, he thought. That's gotta be a first. He got back in the station wagon, behind the wheel. Pomfret had left the key in the ignition. Donahoo could drive away, leave. He wanted to do that, but this was nowhere, no sign of life in any direction, just drifting sand, and at the moment it wasn't drifting. Pomfret, when he came back, might have a problem hitching a ride, no broken down vehicle to show. He might have to walk for miles to the first house.

If he came back, Donahoo thought. He sure couldn't figure Wilson Pomfret. The guy was really curious. He could be up to anything. He could have chosen this spot in advance to vacate. There could be a secondary road on the other side of the dune. There could be a car waiting, a confederate.

Donahoo wondered if he should go take a look. All it meant was getting some sand in his shoes. He thought about it for a while and then he thought he ought to teach Pomfret a lesson. He started the station wagon, bucked across the median, and got back on the freeway, heading west toward San Diego.

He got about two miles down the freeway in still light traffic and decided he was acting as foolishly as Pomfret. He couldn't blame the shanghai on him, not with everybody in on the thing, Lewis, all of

Squad 5. Saperstein also would have given his blessing. Probably DA Davis too. So why blame Pomfret?

He settled in behind a huge semi as they approached a county road overpass. He was going to go back, to make another U on the median, as soon as he got through. He'd talk to Pomfret, he thought. Work something out.

A helicopter, flying fast, flying low, went by on the south side of the freeway, bound for Arizona. It was flying lower than it ought to be so close to traffic. He was trying to read the lettering on the underside, it looked like NEWS, when it made an abrupt turn and lost altitude, as if it might be coming after him.

What the hell? For a moment, he didn't believe it, but then he realized it was closing fast. Instinctively, he hit the gas, moved in front of the semi, and stayed right in front of it, protected by its bulk, until he reached the underpass. Then he jammed the brakes and veered off the pavement. The Chevy almost rolled as it sparked along the wall of concrete. The semi went roaring past with its air horns blaring.

Donahoo stopped a few feet beyond the overpass's cover. The chopper flew over, very low. It started to turn. Donahoo threw the Chevy into reverse. He backed up desperately. The chopper, making its turn, clipped a high tension wire, lost control. It plunged to the ground and exploded in a huge orange fireball.

Sonofabitch. Donahoo drove out from under the overpass. He made a U on the median and drove past the burning wreckage. He slowed at the point where he was within fifty yards of it. There was no way the pilot or anyone on board could have survived. He thought of stopping and decided that wouldn't serve any useful purpose. It would be at least an hour before the mess cooled off. The Highway Patrol would be on the scene long before then. They'd probably object to him sifting through the ashes. He continued back down the freeway.

The V was still at the top of the dune. There were footprints coming down alongside those that had gone up. But there was no sign of Wilson Pomfret. He was gone.

chapter 26

Donahoo crossed the state border, made it to Yuma, Arizona and a place called Jimmy's which was serving a steak and egg breakfast for $3.99. He was still trying to figure Wilson Pomfret. The guy, he had to be under a lot of strain or something, he thought. It didn't make any sense for an FBI agent to abandon a candidate for the Witness Protection Program.

Let's get it straight. It was he, Donahoo, who was supposed to disappear, not Wilson Pomfret. The guy was almost bawling. Would anybody believe that?

Donahoo finished his breakfast and nursed his coffee. He didn't know what the hell to do. He thought that he could still go into the program. He could get a short haircut and dye his hair white. Wear a fake, big, black, bushy mustache till he grew one of his own. Keep on truckin' till he found a place that appealed. But that wasn't really being in the program. That was being out there on his own, without support or backup, if needed. To really be in the program he'd have to cooperate, do what they told him, stay where they wanted. That's probably how it worked.

Next question. If he decided to cooperate, who was he supposed to cooperate with? He didn't fancy making a cold call to the FBI. Uh, listen, I just made one of your agents cry, and I was wondering . . .

Jesus, Donahoo thought. He was in a jam here. The situation back in San Diego had to be pretty bad. He couldn't see it maybe—not as bad as it was. He was too close, too personally involved, but his whole squad, even Cominsky, and Lewis and Saperstein, they obviously all thought the same way, that it was pretty bad back there. They wouldn't have been party to the shanghai otherwise.

It was almost seven o'clock. Lewis would be up by now. Donahoo found the calling card Pomfret had left him. He went to the cafe's pay phone and called Lewis.

He said, "Lewis, one question . . ."

Lewis said, "Tommy, what in the hell is the matter with you, you can't even get kidnapped properly? I just got a call from Pomfret. He was practically crying. He says he got outa the car to take a leak and you drove off. He says he had to walk a mile in the Sand Hills."

"He said that?"

"That's right. A mile."

"Well, he's a liar," Donahoo said. "He didn't have to. I went back. I was just blowing some steam and if he'd shown any patience . . ." He stopped. He couldn't believe he was defending himself. "Did he happen to mention the kamikaze pilot?"

"Huh?"

"I thought not. I was going back down the freeway?—after I left Pomfret?—and a news chopper came after me like a dive bomber. It got tangled in some power lines. Crashed like a bomb. Pomfret didn't mention it?"

"No. How far was this away?"

"From Pomfret? Two miles."

"So what's the question?"

Donahoo tried to think. Maybe Pomfret was too far away to see the fireball. Two miles. Was that too far?

"He didn't see smoke?"

"He didn't see you. That's the problem."

"No. The problem is he went on the other side of a whole fucking sand dune to take a leak."

"Tommy," Lewis said. He sounded like he was really trying to be patient and show understanding. "You're mad at this guy 'cuz he didn't see a chopper crash and wouldn't show you his peepee? Is that what we've got going here? Is this what is bothering you?"

"Look," Donahoo said. "Forget the chopper, okay? We're back to one question. Who really put me on the road out here?"

"The Federal Bureau of Investigation. Do you have a problem with that?"

"Yeah."

"Why?"

"The chopper. I had only just left Pomfret. It was like it was a setup."

"Don't be ridiculous."

"Lewis," Donahoo pleaded. "You've got to help me, okay? There is something radically wrong with this whole situation. I've got a real problem with the FBI."

"Tommy," Lewis said. "If that's true . . ." There was a troubled silence. "Tommy, the FBI is the flag. It's . . ."

Donahoo tried to help him with it. "Motherhood, safe streets, Saturday night, Mary Tyler Moore?"

"If you can't trust the FBI, then I don't know what to tell you, Tommy. I don't know how to help you."

Donahoo said, "Sure, you love me, but . . ."

Lewis, hanging up, said, "Tommy, trust me, wherever you're going, it's not far enough."

"Lewis!"

He was gone.

Donahoo stared at the phone. He couldn't believe Lewis had cut him off. What the hell did Lewis think? That his line wasn't secure? He wondered if it was that bad. He called Cominsky.

"Sarge?" Cominsky yelled, excited. "Where the hell are you? No, don't tell me, my phone could be tapped. Maybe they're tracing the call. You don't know today's technology."

Yeah, that bad, Donahoo thought. He closed his eyes. His headache was coming back.

"Uh. You're not mad at us, are you? Running you off? We did it for your own good. You just couldn't see it. It's real bad here, Sarge. Real bad."

Donahoo was going to complain but didn't have the heart. Cominsky, well, whatever the thought processes, the guy was gold.

"Lewis called. You talk to him yet? He thought you might call me. He wanted to know what the hell you did to Pomfret. He says you really shook him up. I mean, whoa, Sarge. How do you make an FBI agent cry?"

Donahoo thought there had to be a lot of ways. Dig out a picture of J. Edgar Hoover in a garter belt. That ought to be surefire. "He wasn't crying. He was *almost* crying. Is the guy for real? Lewis didn't just pull him outa the air?"

"No. He's the McCoy. Lewis asked the San Diego FBI, who was their best man, hiding a witness, and they recommended Pomfret, highly. They said nobody could touch him. He's outa Washington."

"He's outa marbles."

"He's a veteran. Thirty years."

Donahoo shook his head. He couldn't figure it.

"Sarge. You gotta trust the FBI."

"Sure. Ruby Ridge, Waco."

"Aberrations."

"The crime lab."

"A dereliction."

"Cominsky," Donahoo said, sighing, "how bad is it there?"

"I dunno. I just had to take Lewis's word. He said it was real bad."

"Lewis's word?"

"There's nothing wrong with that, is there?"

"Lewis's?"

"Sarge. He's a captain."

"Of course," Donahoo said. "So everybody else, Gomez, Montrose, Palmer, they all had to take Lewis's word too?"

"Sure. That's okay, isn't it?"

"Of course." Donahoo was trying to think. Who told Lewis it was so freakin' all terrible bad? The FBI. It had to be the FBI. And it was the FBI that brought in Special Agent Wilson Pomfret.

"You still there?"

"Yes. I was just wondering what I ever did to the FBI."

"What did you do?"

Nothing, Donahoo thought. Yet.

"You still there?"

"Yes."

"Well," Cominsky said, "maybe you shouldn't be, Sarge. Maybe you should keep going and not come back for a while. Maybe that's best all round. It's not just Mad Marvin. It's not just Prescott Havershot III. It's also Vickers and Dugan, they're trying to pin Willie Johnson on you, Sarge. That million dollars didn't buy you a day. But you can rest assured I'll be holding the fort. I was going to sublet your place and move in with Oscar. I was just waiting to hear what you planned to do. Also, this may not be my business, but I think it would be a good idea, if you made a clean break with Travata. It can't be love. You've only seen her a few times. You don't wanta jump to conclusions." Cominsky said, "Where you going, Sarge? Don't tell me."

Donahoo went out to the Chevy station wagon. He picked through the gym bag that was one of Pomfret's parting gifts. There were a couple clean shirts and several changes of underwear. A toilet kit. A pair of sneakers. A big black bushy stick-on mustache. No Colt Python. A color brochure. He opened it. He read,

What gives Cairo its magnificent sense of past times is the same thing that threatens its future: decay . . .

Donahoo turned the brochure over to see who had produced that winner. It said, *For further information, contact: CAIRO CHAMBER OF COMMERCE.*

Well, he thought. They couldn't shoot straight, and they were honest. Maybe it wasn't such a bad place after all? He found a real estate flyer with several listings. A three bedroom house for $7,500, another for $13,500. Two houses for $16,000. On six lots with magnolia and oak trees.

Yeah, but the taxes are bitch, right? Donahoo found the highest price asked, $79,500. Charming 14-room home with approx. 4,000 sq ft living space across from beautiful city park and tennis courts. Large hardwood floor entry hall with brick fireplace. Egg and dart dentil pattern in masonry and appropriate pattern framing firebox. He stopped reading when he got to the beveled glass transoms over all the doors and the half-fluted pillars with combination Ionic and Corinthian capitals in the living room. $79,500. That would hardly buy him a parking space in San Diego. There had to be something wrong, *terribly wrong*, with Cairo, Illinois. They were giving the place away. They were signing it over.

Still. Donahoo sneaked another look at the 14-room charmer. It looked ready to go. He might have to dig out a couple of those strange bushes in front. But that's about all. French doors to sunroom. Those beveled glass panes again. Two sun porches. Six-sided oak parquet with patterned border in the downstairs bath. Chair rail in the living room.

Boy. Even Prescott Havershot III's layout in Rancho Santa Fe didn't have some of this stuff. Donahoo studied the photo. The house was attractive but not pretentious. He could picture himself hiding out in it for a year or so. He wouldn't have to mix all that much with the local citizenry. If necessary, he could stay inside, watch television, have groceries delivered. He read some more of the copy. Large ginko tree, magnolias. Large lot runs from one street to another. Drive-through garage. Well, that almost settled it, Donahoo thought. It was tailor-made for him. Drive-through garage to another street. Perfect for getaways.

He went back to the pay phone in Jimmy's and called the San Diego public library and asked for Reference. He said, "I was wondering what you could tell me about Cairo, Illinois?"

The woman clerk went away for a while and when she got back, she said, "Would you like to hear what Charles Dickens said about it?"

He said, "The writer?"

She said, "Yes."

He said, "Okay."

She said, "Here goes." She said Dickens had passed through in April, 1842, when Cairo claimed two thousand inhabitants, and that she was quoting Dickens's impressions, as published in his *American Notes*.

" 'At the junction of the two rivers, on ground so flat and low and marshy that at certain seasons of the year it is inundated to the house-tops, lies a breeding-place of fever, ague, and death . . . ' "

Donahoo said, "Wait a minute. Have we got the right place?"

She said, "Yes, Cairo, Illinois," and continued.

" 'A dismal swamp, on which the half-built houses rot away; cleared here and there for a space of a few yards; and teeming, then, with rank and unwholesome vegetation, in whose baleful shade the wretched wanderers who are tempted hither, droop, and die, and lay their bones.' "

Donahoo said, "Lady, Jesus . . ."

She said, " 'The hateful Mississippi circling and eddying before it, and turning off upon its southern course a slimy monster hideous to behold; a hotbed of disease, an ugly sepulchre, a grave uncheered by any gleam of promise.' "

"Lady . . ."

" 'A place without one single quality, in earth or air or water, to commend it. Such is this dismal Cairo.' "

Donahoo said, "Thanks, I think I've got a fix on it."

She said, "I have a Chamber of Commerce color brochure here. It presents a little more upbeat picture of the decay."

He thanked her again and hung up. Hold on, he thought. Hold fucking on. There was something radically wrong here. This was a town so bad that one of the greatest figures in literature took the trouble to piss on it. Here was a town so bad that even the Chamber of Commerce was negative. So why would FBI Special Agent Wilson Pomfret suggest that anyone settle in Cairo in the Witness Protection Program?

Because . . .

Donahoo pushed back into the station wagon. Because nobody in their right mind would do it, he thought. They'd refuse. They'd tell Promfet to get stuffed. Pomfret would feign hurt.

And? Donahoo dropped the "they." He inserted himself into the equation. There'd be a big foofaraw. A couple of big egos would get separated. Pomfret would go crying to Lewis. He, Donahoo, would suddenly be on his own, out in the open, far from home . . . and?

Donahoo looked at his watch. He had wasted a couple of hours. If it was unfolding the way he had it figured, he could afford to waste another, he thought. It would take them that long to get back on his trail. To react to the chopper crash. To get another bird in the air. To get it out here. Besides, they wouldn't be in any big rush, relying on—how had Cominsky put it—today's technology.

Down the road a ways there was a small auto wrecking operation, it looked Mexican, there was a sign, MEXREK Auto Destruccion. It was a one-man operation. The guy spoke a little English. He called himself Dismantler Miguel.

Donahoo gave him two hundred dollars to take the Chevy station wagon apart—while he watched.

"While you watch, Senõr?" Miguel asked, he wanted to make sure he had that correctly, and Donahoo, in answer, dragged over an old armchair and sat down.

It took about an hour. By this time the Chevy was in many pieces. The seats had been removed. The roof liner and upholstery had been stripped away. Only the block was left intact under the hood. Miguel, on his third visit to the undercarriage, emerged with a gas filter that wasn't a gas filter, but actually a cleverly disguised little box which, upon close examination, looked suspiciously like a transmitter of some sort.

"Well, what do you think?" Donahoo said. "Would you say that's a beeper? Like the device used to locate a downed pilot?"

Miguel shrugged elaborately.

"Do you think it can be turned on and off?"

Miguel smiled acknowledgment. He pointed to what he thought was a switch. With Donahoo's permission, he turned it off, then handed it over.

Donahoo pocketed it and capped the bottle of Old Crow he had bought in the drugstore next to Jimmy's. He asked to use the phone. He wanted to call a cab.

Miguel asked, "What do you want me to do with the car, Senõr?"

Donahoo told him, "I think you should dismantle it, Dismantler Miguel."

chapter 27

San Diego. Donahoo thought it was weird being a stranger in his own town. He'd left as Tommy Donahoo, and he was coming back as Jersey Myers. He'd gotten a haircut, very short for him, while waiting for the Greyhound in Yuma. When he'd finished, the barber had said, "George Clooney, that's what you were trying for, huh?"

Donahoo had said, "What were *you* trying for?"

He'd rubbed some white shoe polish on it. Temporary till he figured something better. He'd stuck on the big black bushy mustache. He'd sprung for a pair of aviator sunglasses, they turned the world away, made it look orange/lemon/grapefruit, he could have his pick.

He got off the bus feeling very much alone and a little afraid. He'd made up his mind he wasn't going to tell anyone he was in San Diego. That was too risky. Word would get around. It would get back. Eventually, it would get to Saperstein, to Lewis, and since they knew better, or thought they did, it would get to the FBI.

Donahoo thought again that he had a real problem with the FBI. The flag and Mary Tyler Moore. A casket for a cop who knew too much. Maybe yes and maybe no. Too close to call. Too close to piss around with.

Instead of entering the bus depot, he turned his jacket collar up, cut across the back lot to Front Street, walked the few blocks up Broadway to the Downtown YMCA. He was traveling light, using the gym bag Pomfret had packed for him.

The *Union-Tribune*'s late street edition was in the box in front of the Y. He bought a copy thinking there was a chance it might have something about the chopper. There was no mention of it. The *Union-Tribune*'s last deadline, for some reason, seemed to be earlier than its first deadline. It had something to do with the merger of the *Union* and the *Tribune*. No more newspaper competition except from the weekly *Reader*. This was the first time it annoyed him though. Normally he didn't mind getting his bad news late.

He found a pay phone in the Y's lobby and called the KFMB Channel 8 newsroom. He got a reporter named Karen.

He said, "This is the San Diego Police Department. We're comparing notes here. The chopper crash this morning off I-8 in Imperial County. Do you have confirmation it was a news chopper?"

Karen sounded puzzled. "No. We've got it as a private aircraft without a point of origin. What have you got?"

"I asked first."

"What you've got," she said, suspicious now. "One dead, the pilot, not identified. No passengers." There was a pause. "Can't you get this from the sheriff's office?"

"I'm saving the taxpayers a long-distance toll. What have you got on a possible bomb?"

"Yeah," she said slowly. "We heard that. The explosion and fire pretty much demolished it." Another pause. "Listen, why don't you give me your name, I'll let you know if there's anything new, I can't have too many contacts in the police department."

He was stuck. He said, "Cominsky." He gave her Cominsky's voice mail number.

Donahoo hung up thinking that he really couldn't do this alone. He needed help. At least one guy. He'd already chosen him.

Cominsky.

He bought a Y day pass and spent a couple hours losing himself. He worked out in the weight room. Ran several miles on the indoor track above the basketball court. Chalked up several more miles in the pool. Did the sauna. The spa. Had a steam. Stood in a hot shower forever.

He came out feeling better but no closer to a solution.

How to run from the FBI?

Well, there were guys who did it, he thought. The guys on the wanted posters in the post office. So it could be done. For a while anyway. And maybe that's all he needed. Some time.

He didn't think he had much. He used to be king of the hill. Now, when he closed his eyes, he was king of a sand castle, and the tide was coming in.

Donahoo found Cominsky at the AmVets thrift store in Middletown. Cominsky was trying on a tan raincoat that was a couple sizes too big for him. Too loose at the shoulders and too long in the sleeves. It didn't do anything for him.

Donahoo whispered, "Hello, Cominsky." Cominsky, reacting with wide eyes, slack jaw, said, "Holy shit!"

"It's okay," Donahoo said softly. "Just a bad haircut. A dye job." He checked to make sure the big bushy black mustache was still in place. "I'm in disguise."

Cominsky sighed with relief. "Gawd. I thought you might have turned gray overnight or something—all the strain you've been under." He squeezed against the raincoat rack to let a fellow shopper pass. "How the hell did you find me?"

Donahoo shrugged, as if it was merely luck, not a foregone conclusion. Wednesday was Cominsky's day off and, not by coincidence, Senior's Day at the Middletown AmVet, half price on all clothes, shoes, linens, books and miscellaneous, except for a certain color price tag, which, on this day, was blue. So Cominsky was either going to be here, checking out all the other-than-blue tags, or at the Bowl-a-rama, zapping the cooties out of any shoes he may have found to his liking.

"What the hell are you doing in San Diego?"

Donahoo hesitated. It was too late to change his mind but it still worried him that he was taking such a big chance with Cominsky. He was going to throw in with him. Tell him everything. Put his life in his hands. The upside was that no one would ever believe that he'd trust Cominsky to such an extent. Saperstein, Lewis, it wouldn't enter their minds. Gomez, Montrose, Palmer, they'd laugh at the idea. The downside was that Cominsky could get him killed without trying.

"You're supposed to be . . ." Cominsky looked around the vast hangar-like shed that housed the Middletown AmVet. The place was packed with shoppers but no one was paying attention. They were all intent on their bargain hunting. ". . . hiding your ass, Sarge."

Donahoo shushed him. "Don't call me that, you idiot."

Cominsky flushed. "Sorry." He looked around again. "Uh, what am I supposed to call you?"

Donahoo didn't know. He had thought about it but had been un-able to decide. It would take time to come up with a new identity and a new disguise. He wasn't sure he had any time to spare. So he was tempted to continue with the identity given him by Pomfret. It protected him, at least at a distance, from recognition by his squad members, other cops. But it was a giveaway if he encountered Pom-fret. He couldn't afford to be recognized by the Pelican Man. Not for a while, anyway. He had information to collect.

Plans to formulate. Things to do.

"Jersey," he said finally. It was the easy solution. Maybe not the right one. "Jersey Myers. Jersey as in the state."

"The *new* Jersey, huh?" Cominsky said, winking to punctuate the pun. "Is that M-Y-E-R-S? Wait a minute. You sound like The Mob."

This was the man with whom he was placing his life, Donahoo thought. "It's better than sounding like a cop."

"You mean it's part of the disguise?"

"I guess so."

Cominsky let out a low whistle. "That Pomfret. He's pretty smart."

"Yeah. Now can we get outa here?"

"In a minute." Cominsky moved over in front of a narrow wall mirror to check out his raincoat. He looked at himself head-on and then both profiles. He asked, smiling at his image, "What do you think?"

Donahoo didn't have the heart to tell him. He was in a 44T. It was too big by several sizes. He didn't look like Humphrey Bogart.

"Nicholson of St. Albans," Cominsky said, flashing the label. "Made in England. All cotton. Rain resistant, durable proof. Dry cleaning recommended." He unbuttoned the front. "The buttons sewed onto—see the inside?—smaller buttons." He lifted the collar. "The hook you hang it on with? A *metal chain,* not a cloth ribbon. We're talking quality here." He showed the blue price tag. It was marked $9.95. "Five bucks."

"You're still pulling that, huh?"

"Hey, it's part of the tradition," Cominsky said.

He rebuttoned the raincoat and postured before the mirror. "I keep telling you. Seniors don't buy things. They've already got everything they need. They've had their whole life to accumulate. That's not what Senior's Day is all about."

Donahoo looked around. The usual large number of seniors was present. When Cominsky had first brought him here he had thought they were present legitimately. Actually they were here to enter into a criminal conspiracy with non-seniors. Slip them an extra buck and they'd buy what you wanted at half price and then give it to you outside.

"I still say it's taking money from the vets."

"Maybe, but it's giving it to the seniors. It's their day, Sarge, I mean, Jersey. This is Senior's Day."

Donahoo gave up. He said, "It doesn't fit, Cominsky."

Cominsky, looking at him oddly, said, "At these prices, who the hell cares?"

They drove over to Cominsky's flat in the Tamarisk Apartments on Upas on Bankers Hill. In order to be with Oscar, Cominsky had already moved into his, Donahoo's, studio in The Arlington, which was only a couple of miles away from Bankers Hill, on the other side of Hillcrest, in Uptown. So it made sense for Donahoo to simply move into Cominsky's place.

Donahoo was making a list of the things he'd need from The Arlington. A couple suits, shirts, ties, underwear, socks. Another pair of brogans and some sneakers. He'd like his TV. Cominsky didn't have a TV. Donahoo thought he'd also like his slippers. A book he was reading, *The Mad Among Us*. His coffee. Cominsky didn't drink coffee. He drank wheat grass.

The spices. Donahoo put them down. Cominsky didn't have spices. He had garlic.

"Cairo, huh?" Cominsky was saying. He was wearing his raincoat even though it wasn't raining. "So that's what first made you suspicious?"

"Finally convinced me," Donahoo said, a minor correction, but nonetheless important. Everything was important. He wondered if Cominsky was ever going to get anything right the first time. "It was like, you know, the guy was purposely trying to provoke me."

"So as to start a fight?"

"More an argument."

"Right. So Pomfret stops the car, gets out, says he needs to go, takes cover behind the sand dune."

Donaho grunted and tried to get into a more comfortable position. Cominsky's Morris Minor woodie station wagon wouldn't accept his bulk. He felt like he'd been canned.

"You're a sitting duck," Cominsky continued. "Any moment, the chopper is gonna come along, drop a bomb on you. But you're so pissed at Pomfret, you drive away, don't give 'em the chance. The chopper comes looking for you, gets tangled up in the high wires, kaboom." He glanced at Donahoo. "I dunno. It's suspicious, alright. But I don't think you can convict a guy for going to the toilet."

"There's the other stuff," Donahoo protested. He patted the pocket holding the transmitter. "The beeper disguised as a gas filter? The fact that Pomfret got a ride out of the Sand Hills so fast?"

Cominsky looked doubtful. "There's no proof Pomfret put the beeper in the Chevy. No proof he had anything to do with the chopper following you. No proof that getting a quick ride was anything but innocent. You've got him for going to the toilet, that's all."

"I've got him for Cairo."

Cominsky shook his head. "Naw. That could be just real smart on his part. Who the hell would think you'd end up in Little Egypt? It's the last place anybody would think of looking. So maybe that makes it the best?"

"No." Donahoo was sure of it. Pomfret had done it to provoke him. He thought that ought to be pretty plain even to Cominsky. It was the crux of his whole case against the Pelican Man. If he didn't have that, he didn't have much. Cominsky was right about the other things. No proof. He said, "Put a cork in it. He did it to provoke me."

Cominsky shrugged. He changed the subject. "There's a couple things I need you to do for me. Don't use the garbage disposal. There's a reminder above the sink. That stuff now goes in the Little Heap Composter."

Oh, fuck, Donahoo thought. His nerves were raw. He wished he was doing this on his own. It looked like Cominsky was a big mistake. He said, "That dumb fucking thing . . ." and was immediately sorry, but it was too late.

"Yeah, well, maybe it's like you coming to me for help, Jersey, " Cominsky said, staring straight ahead. "Who'd ever think you'd do a dumb thing like that. So maybe that's why it's a good idea?" He was still looking straight ahead. "Just because it's so dumb."

"Uh," Donahoo said. He felt terrible. He didn't know what to say. "Listen. I'm relying on you, for chrissakes. You check your voice mail you'll probably find a message from a newsgal at Channel 8. Karen. I asked her to give you anything new she might get on that chopper."

"Why don't you just watch the news?"

"Because it might be something unconfirmed that they don't want to put on the air."

"You believe that?"

"Goddamn," Donahoo started to say, then caught himself. He didn't want to hurt Cominsky's feelings any more than he already had. "Listen, you, uh, don't need to bring me all that much from my place, okay? Just some clothes, and my record player, that record, 'I Wonder Who's Kissing Her Now.'" He tried to think. "You might want to bring me any that's left of the Old Crow."

Cominsky, he was still looking straight ahead, replied, "I don't know how you can drink that poison, Jersey."

Donahoo told him, "Yeah, well, if you eat any more of that kale, we can get you a role on *Star Trek*—Jerko from the planet Bonko. You goddamn pain in the ass."

chapter 28

Cominsky's flat. Donahoo thought that it was flat alright. It was carpet-bombing level. The word was Spartan. It had no varoom. He stood in the back doorway, listening to Cominsky's Morris Minor eggbeat up the alley, bound for better, more lavish digs. His. He thought he always knew this place was primitive. It just hadn't registered all that well. He had never thought of living in it.

He dropped the gym bag and pulled the door shut behind him. The upside—lately he was always looking for the upside—the upside was he wouldn't be staying very long. He was going to get the bad guys or they were going to get him.

He was in the kitchen. It was painted in sickroom green. Bare, mottled, worn linoleum. A sink and a couple cupboards. An old fridge and an older gas stove. A wooden table and two wooden chairs.

He found the light switch. Overhead, a low-watt single bulb, dimmed further by its bowl cover, flickered uncertainly.

Over the sink there was a big framed picture of a cartoon hippo sitting in a child's blow-up pool. It was crooked. He tried to straighten it, and it wouldn't budge. It seemed to be nailed flat, but there were no nails. Nearby was a jar of goop labeled LIFETIME GUARAN-TEE NEVER-FALL-OFF STICKUM.

He sighed. One of Cominsky's inventions. He put the jar in a bin that for some reason also required a label. It said, TOOLS. It held most everything that might be required by the home inventor. Lots of cordless equipment. Cominsky had trouble tripping over cords. There was another bin, FASTENERS. It had every kind imaginable. Nails, eyehooks, clothespins. Donahoo transferred the lifetime guaranteed never-fall-off stickum from TOOLS to FASTENERS. He wanted to be a thoughtful guest.

The Little Heap Composter was next to the drainboard. Donahoo read the sign about what went in the Little Heap.

WHAT GOES IN THE LITTLE HEAP
Everything That Would Normally
Go In the Garbage Disposal
Plus Large Bones

Notes from Cominsky to himself. Donahoo wondered if they were something like Postcards From the Edge. Postcards from *over* the edge. Cominsky claimed he never had a lady here. He always went to her place. So why the instructions?

Donahoo tried to find a rational explanation. Maybe Cominsky was just prepared for the inevitable? Someday, somehow, he was going to wangle a second date, and the woman was going to insist that she come here, see his place. You can't know a man until you inspect his kitchen. Maybe that was it?

He checked the fridge. Fruit juice. Vegetable juice. No beer. A bin full of carrots, spinach, broccoli, kale, sweet potatoes. No food. He checked the cupboards. Several varieties of spaghetti, bran flakes. No canned goods except tomato paste. No food. He went under the sink. No alcohol.

Donahoo retrieved the gym bag. He was not going to be happy here, he thought. This was not a home. It was a laboratory. They were trying to determine if man could survive without pleasure.

The living room, which was also the bedroom, was as bare as the kitchen. There was a futon which was also the bed. Homemade wooden bookshelves on all the walls. Mostly paperback books. Mostly self-help stuff.

Donahoo checked a few titles. *Selections from Overcoming Hypertension. The Disowned Self. When Bad Things Happen to Good People. Be Fit as a Marine.* Jesus. Donahoo wondered what he was supposed to read. There wasn't a TV. He went along a whole shelf. *What You Think of Me Is None of My Business. Maximum Metabolism. Are You Confused? Doctor Morrison's Miracle Guide to Pain-Free Health and Longevity.*

Finally he chose *Lifesaving, Rescue and Water Safety.* He was going under, he thought. For the third time.

He stretched out on the futon with the gym bag as a pillow.

He read: *"Human beings do not naturally belong in the water. Their whole physical makeup has been developed for terrestrial living."* Next page. *"Many types of swimming areas exist, from the old swimming hole to the modern natatorium."* Next page. *"Sharks, barracudas, moray eels, and other predators all can produce severe bite wounds. The best protection is not to swim in areas where aquatic predators are present."*

Donahoo sighed and put the book aside. He wondered what the fuck a natatorium was. He was going to have to get serious here, he thought. Get his old eye on the old ball. Focus.

He closed, a contradiction, his eyes. He let the sand castle image dissolve. Let the incoming tide recede. Let go of the idea that the whole Federal Bureau of Investigation wanted him, Donahoo, off the planet. Let go of the idea that Havershot was a demented greedy pig who would go to any extreme to make his daughter skip jumping.

He let it all go, and then it seemed so simple, and then it got complicated, and then it got very complicated. He tried to arrange his varied suspicions in some semblance of order. If he could eliminate Havershot, or at least get him down on the list, maybe he could risk calling Travata. He sure hoped so. He missed her a lot. Now there's a lady, he thought. She jumps when you call. He was feeling a little giddy. He made the list.

The Pelican Man is a rogue cop. He's working for Mad Marvin.

He puts the beeper under the Chevy, or lets one of Mad Marvin's goons do it. Anyway, at the appointed spot, the appointed time, he ditches the Chevy, goes over the dune. The chopper comes along and drops a bomb on the beeper. Mad Marvin's problem is solved.

Neat?

No, Donahoo thought. It was messy. They didn't need a chopper. People would notice a chopper. They'd report seeing or hearing an explosion and seeing or hearing a chopper, and a chopper is a lot easier to trace than a car. It would be better to use a car. On a freeway a car can track a beeper just as readily as a chopper. It can catch up and drift by, and the hit can be accomplished with guns. You saw it in the movies all the fucking time. So why the overkill? Mad Marvin may be nuts, but Pomfret wasn't. Why would Pomfret put himself anywhere near where somebody is going to drop a bomb?

Next scenario. Pomfret isn't working for Mad Marvin. He's working for Prescott Havershot. But the question persists, why would Pomfret agree to a bomb?

Next scenario. Pomfret doesn't agree. They double-cross him—Mad Marvin or Havershot—one or the other.

Next scenario. Pomfret is working for both Mad Marvin and Havershot.

Next scenario. Pomfret is working for one of them and the other horns in on the kill, unbeknownst to him.

Donahoo sat up. He knew he liked one of them, but he wasn't sure which. One of the last two. The last?

Yeah. He thought that maybe the horning-in idea made the most sense. He kicked it around, and he definitely liked it best.

The way it went was this: Pomfret works for The Mob. It's planned as a clean hit. No need for a beeper. Pomfret tells The Mob where he'll be and when. He stops the Chevy, gets out, takes cover. The Mob is supposed to come by and bang, bang. Only trouble is the Chevy is gone. Headed west.

Enter the Havershot phenomenon, existing apart from, and unbeknownst to, The Mob. One of Havershot's minions has planted the beeper. Another of his minions is flying the chopper. It locates him,

Donahoo. When he takes evasive action the pilot maneuvers blindly and tangles in the high wires.

Donahoo thought it was perfect. It explained how Pomfret got out of there so quickly. The Mob hit car picked him up. It explained why they lost him, Donahoo. They weren't tracking a beeper. All The Mob had was his tire marks in the median, heading back west.

Yes, he thought. It all made sense. They went after him the wrong way. They passed each other going in opposite directions. The Mob missed him.

Yes, yes, *yes!* That's how it happened. Two hits, not one, and they bungled both of them, because he, Donahoo, was a very lucky cop.

He opened his eyes. He wondered why he was so pleased with himself. He had met the enemy—and it was everybody?

He backtracked. If there was a flaw, it was a big one, Prescott Havershot III. He had not been taking him as a serious threat and now he was. Which should it be? Often, when a guy threatened to kill you, he was serious. Not always, but often, often enough. All joking aside, and there had been a lot of jokes on the subject, all at his expense, Havershot had threatened him personally and repeated it to Saperstein. Sure, he was angry, sure, he was throwing his weight around, but still, wasn't it foolhardy to ignore him?

Yes and no, Donahoo thought, uncertain. In this day and age, angry fathers did not kill unwanted suitors. Besides, he wasn't even a suitor, they'd just made a couple of jumps together. So where, really, was the motive?

Donahoo tried to figure it. Tried to think of who he could go to for help. He remembered Lewis's first piece of advice. See a lawyer.

Gawd, he thought. He didn't want to see any of the lawyers he knew. He'd rather see O'Malley. He'd rather let O'Malley pat his knee than see a lawyer. Hell, he'd rather sit on O'Malley's knee than see a lawyer. Still, Lewis was right. He had to do it.

chapter 29

Malcolm Philpott, of Herzog, Garfield & Philpott. The lawyer who handled Travata's trust. The shark.

Donahoo took a walk to the 7-Eleven at Fifth and Spruce. He bought a couple *Auto Traders,* one with ads for old American models, prior to 1991, the other European, all years. The Toronado was in pieces. The Chevy was in parts. Tomorrow he was going to have to buy a car.

There was a pay phone. He called Herzog, Garfield & Philpott and got a live answering service. He gave his name and said he would like to be patched through to Philpott. He said he would wait for thirty seconds.

Philpott was on the line in twenty. He said, "*The* Tommy Dona-hoo?"

Donahoo said, "Can we meet somewhere? It might be mutually advantageous."

Philpott asked, "When?"

Donahoo said, "Now."

They made the arrangements.

"Start driving," Donahoo said. "Where are you now? Point Loma.

Okay. Head downtown. I'll get settled—somewhere I'm happy?—and I'll call you in your car to finalize. You got a cellular?" Then he said, "Need I mention it? Come alone."

Philpott gave his cellular number. He said he'd be driving a sable black Cadillac convertible, a 1984 Biarritz. He said the top would be down. He said, "I haven't done this in years."

Donahoo said, "I've never done it."

Donahoo took a taxi downtown. He was hungry. He hadn't eaten since breakfast, so he dropped off at Rubio's, a fish taco place which was across the street, on an angle, from the Fourth Avenue parking entrance to the Horton's Plaza shopping complex. He made another pay phone call and reached Philpott on his cellular. He told him Horton's Plaza. Park there.

Philpott still sounded cool. He said, "I'm tall, dark and successful. How will I recognize you?"

Donahoo said, "I'll have a rose in my teeth." He was going to say a fish taco but he wasn't cool. He was nervous. Philpott could be in cahoots with Havershot. You never know, he thought. You never, ever know.

The Biarritz drifted by about ten minutes later. Philpott had been right about one thing. He was successful. The convertible was a collector's dream. Like new, super clean, just over 2,000 made. Come check it out.

Donahoo reluctantly left his tacos and went back to the pay phone.

"Let's go for a walk," he said. "South on Fourth. Bring the cellular."

"Understood."

Donahoo returned to Rubio's. A few minutes later Philpott exited Horton's Plaza via the parking entrance, on foot, as instructed. He wasn't as tall as advertised. Average build, actually. And not particularly attractive. Protruding eyes and a cat's mouth in a ruddy round head with light brown thinning hair clinging to it. An English tradesman type aspiring to be upper class. Nothing special about him except the long dark overcoat too warm for the weather. A long white scarf. It would blow with the top down. Fighter pilot stuff. He started south.

"Shark, huh? More like a pussy." Donahoo was talking to himself.

He waited awhile and then followed on the opposite side of the street. "Here, pussy, pussy."

Two more calls to Philpott's cellular. One at Market. The second at K Street. Donahoo was happy. No trouble in sight.

Then, finally, at the Trolley stop across from the Convention Center, a last call to Philpott, who was thirty feet away now, looking expectantly at the Trolley for Tijuana. "Board."

Philpott had to run for it. Donahoo boarded with him.

The Trolley lurched away. There were only a few other passengers in their car. A young couple, they looked like students, they had backpacks, books. An old woman laden with plastic bags filled with vegetables from the Farmers Bazaar. Two sullen hoods in gang attire who immediately moved to the rear.

"Frankly," Philpott said, wiping off a seat with a handkerchief. He was looking at Donahoo. He pursed his cat's mouth. "I don't see the attraction."

Donahoo hoped that was prompted in part by the dye job and phony mustache. But then again he hadn't understood the attraction either. Not from the first moment. She should have picked the aerospace engineer.

"But then there's no understanding women, is there?" Philpott continued. He was still looking critically at Donahoo. "Amazing."

"Right. Travata has discussed our, uh, relationship, I assume?"

"Which brings me here," Philpott said. He indicated that Donahoo should sit across from him. "For some odd reason, she likes you, Sergeant. She thinks she's in love."

Donahoo sat down slowly. He didn't wipe the seat off. His neck felt hot. He said, "We've, uh, only been out a couple times."

"Out?"

"That's what I call it."

"Well, it sounds like in to me," Philpott complained. He took another look at Donahoo. Shook his head in disbelief. "This is preposterous."

"Uh," Donahoo said. "If it doesn't fuck with attorney/client privilege, maybe you could tell me, is your client, uh, mentally impaired to, uh, any significant degree?"

"You'd think so, wouldn't you?" Philpott said seriously. "But actually, no."

"Mr. Havershot said . . ."

"He's a lying snake."

Donahoo leaned back. He didn't know how to take Philpott's news. Miss Pussy-in-the-Sky was in love with him? And she *wasn't* unbalanced?!!

"Travata told you about the trust?" Philpott asked. "Her father essentially manages it for her. She gets everything when she's thirty?"

"Yes."

"What she may not have mentioned, and you will appreciate her reluctance, sir: If she marries, she gets it all, immediately."

Donahoo felt his blood quicken. He'd been looking for a decent motive for Havershot. He seemed to have found it. "Right away?"

"Yes. Now." Philpott glanced at the sullen hoods at the end of the car. He lowered his voice. "Needless to say, we are speaking of many millions of dollars, Sergeant. A vast fortune. Kept intact by rigid rules. Havershot controls it but derives little benefit from it. And, with two little words, 'I do,' it disappears. He's left nothing, dependent on Travata's good nature."

Donahoo couldn't believe any of it. "How can that be? Surely Havershot has salted something away over the years?"

Philpott shook his head. "No. The trust is extremely onerous. It demands that he *increase* its value annually or lose control. I step in. He's just been barely able to meet his quota. Hardly anything left over. So he's in a bind. Five years remaining to build a decent nestegg. Or, what really shakes him, if Travata marries, he's broke."

"Broke?"

"Yes. Totally dependent on a child who is deservedly pissed at him. He finds the mere thought traumatic. So perhaps that explains the hysterics when a suitor arrives?"

Philpott looked around. Lowered his voice again. "I agreed to this meeting out of conscience. There is something you should know. He hated you the moment he saw you."

Yes, well, but he only saw me on the fly, Donahoo thought. He tried to diminish the jeopardy. "What about the big house in Rancho Santa Fe?"

"He doesn't own it. He's *buying* it, like the rest of us. No equity of consequence. Probably none. He bought at the peak. He's barely managed to hold on to it."

"That explains his mean office in the Spreckles?"

"Partially. The main reason is he's a fruitcake. He claims Travata is emotionally challenged? He's overwhelmed. He's been courting disaster for years. He never got along with the managers of the various companies he controls. They kept quitting. There was no continuity. So he decided to work at a distance from them. His poor surroundings are meant to signal economy of operation. An example. What can I say?"

Donahoo still couldn't believe it. The Trolley stopped. The young couple got off. The old lady with the vegetables got off.

"Well," Philpott said. "That's my side of it. There are some obvious conclusions to be drawn. A, I'm not against Travata marrying you, although, frankly, I'm appalled at her choice. If she marries I get wealthy administering, *intelligently,* her vast holdings, five years ahead of schedule. B, I can wait. I've got a successful law practice, a big house in Point Loma, a boat in the harbor and my nose in the air. I don't want or need to get involved in a premature bid for the trust funds. C, I don't feel comfortable commenting on the unseemly disappearance of fiancé Erskine Fotheringham, nor the unfortunate demise of Maxwell 'Tiger' Barr. I trust you were listening carefully. Now, what was it that you wished to say?"

"Who?" Donahoo asked, meaning Barr. He was new.

"Another candidate."

"For what?"

"Six feet of God's good earth. Except his body was never located. That's all I'm going to say on the subject. If you want more information, get it yourself, detective."

Donahoo thought he was bleeding and that it was all his fault. He had been warned, and he hadn't paid attention. He'd gone swimming in shark-infested waters. He said, "Havershot. Is he desperate enough to kill me?"

Philpott stood up. He smiled. "Attorney-client privilege."

The Trolley slowed to stop. Donahoo glanced back at the hoods. They were sort of half-decided to get off. They might get off or they might not get off. It all depended, apparently, and they had a long way to make up their minds, lots of stops where they could grab a guy's wallet and wristwatch and leave him by the tracks while they rode on down. National City. Chula Vista. San Ysidro.

"I wouldn't get off yet. I'd ride the whole way."

Philpott said, "To Tijuana? Why?"

Donahoo said, "It's safer."

The Trolley stopped. Philpott got off. The hoods remained on board with Donahoo.

It must be the gray hair, he thought. He must look old, tired, easy. He wondered if he was starting to lose it.

"There was a time," he said loudly, "I coulda made a daisy chain out of you punks. Noses up assholes."

They rode in silence to the next stop. Donahoo got off alone. He guessed he must have made a mistake. Maybe they were students like the couple with the backpacks. Yeah, that was it. Visiting scholars.

Later, back at Cominsky's, Donahoo found a package on the rear stoop. A change of clothes, *'I Wonder Who's Kissing Her Now,'* the record player to play it on, an almost empty bottle of Old Crow, and a curt note about the chopper.

> KAREN SAYS BIG MYSTERY
> NO ID ON BODY OR AIRCRAFT
> LOOKS LIKE YOU'RE SHIT OUTA LUCK.

Cominsky was still pissed.

Well, who wasn't? Donahoo wondered. A beautiful young rich woman falls in love with him, not, of course, that she actually was, or, probably, not that she actually even thought she was, but either way immediately he's marked for death, what kinda karma was that?

It wasn't true. He knew that. He'd bet anything she was just blowing smoke rings up Philpott's shark ass. If it was true, if Travata wanted to marry just anybody, just so she could get her hands on all that money, she was going to have to propose to him, he thought. He sure wasn't going to propose to her. If she did propose, he was going to say no.

He put on the record. He decided to skip the chilled glass. He retired to the futon with the Old Crow and his *Auto Traders*. He needed a car. He thought he'd sure like to get a sable black convertible Biarritz. Here was something. An '84 Peugeot. Vry rlbl.

chapter 30

Travata Havershot. She limped through Donahoo's dreams and made him uneasy. She loved him? He didn't think so. They'd met by chance and had been together twice. Two brief encounters. Two fancy, fantasy, five-star fornications. Maximum copulation and minimum conversation. But love? No. She hadn't had enough time to fall in love. She hadn't had enough time to take off her boots. So what had possessed her to say it?

Donahoo could think of only one reason—to scare the crap out of Prescott Havershot III. To make Havershot think she was marriage-minded and that he was going to lose it all. But why put that kind of pressure on the guy? What did it accomplish? On the surface, all it did, it seemed, was to provoke Havershot into threatening him, Donahoo. How did that in any way help her? What was the payoff?

When he asked the question, 'Why harm me?' another question naturally arose. 'Why frame me for Willie's murder?' He couldn't keep them separate. The Willie Johnson frame seemed too subtle for The Mob. It seemed to have . . . what? A woman's touch?

He hated himself for those kind of questions, but they wouldn't go away. Initially Travata had been a minor suspect. It was why, one of the reasons, he had taken her to the lime green Victorian in Golden Hill. Now, if not a major suspect, she was a major source of irritation, because there was something wrong here, she was getting him into trouble for no apparent reason. He knew only one kind of person who would do that. A spoiled brat. A spoiled rich brat. He'd been hoping for something better.

Donahoo sighed. It was tough trying to carry out an investigation while on the run from not-quite-identified assassins. He couldn't stand still long enough to get a proper fix on anything. It was all loose ends and all dead-ends. Dead-end on the chopper. Dead-end on the car bomb. Dead-end on the million dollars. That left Willie Johnson. There was no dead-end there. Vickers and Dugan hadn't taken that road far enough. They were happy with him, Donahoo. They didn't want any other suspects.

Donahoo decided that he ought to go see Clancy Holden. Maybe she had learned something about Willie. Maybe she knew where he kept the rest of his money, if there was any. Maybe they could get their hands on some of it.

He counted his remaining resources. He was down to about fifteen hundred dollars. He really couldn't afford to keep taking cabs. Cabs were killers. $1.80 a mile. $10 an hour to wait. That was madness. He knew guys who got paid $5 an hour to work.

There was no avoiding it any longer. He was going to have to buy a car.

He found his way into the kitchen. Cominsky was there, having arrived quiet as a mouse, and making, of all things, coffee. He also wanted to make peace. Otherwise he'd be making tea. Herbal tea.

Donahoo thought he'd go along. He needed some help. He said, "Good morning, here's a list. The bomb, the chopper, the mattress money—what's the latest on them? Check around, see what you can find out, okay?" He said, "Vickers and Dugan or Internal Affairs—which is trying to pin Willie Johnson on me?" He waited for some indication that Cominsky planned to take the list. Then he said, "Maxwell 'Tiger' Barr. He's dead. Maybe you can dig up an obit?"

"Uh," Cominsky said finally. "What are you gonna be doing?"

"Buying a car."

He found the Peugeot ad in the *Auto Trader,* European, All Years. It was in the back, in the section headed ALL OTHERS. It said: '1984 Peugeot 505STI, French taxicab, 4cyl, 5spd, AC, PS, PB, xlnt trnsp, vry rlbl, runs good, fntstc mileage, orig paint/owner, $800 obo. Call anytime.'

He decided it sounded pretty good. He showed it to Cominsky. What did he think? Cominsky made a face. He mumbled something about raising one's sights and buying, if necessary, on the installment plan.

Donahoo took the coffee maker away from him. He got it going. He told himself not to argue.

He went back and sat down with Cominsky who was drooling over a 1976 MG Midget, 'stored for last 8 years, 44,000 orig miles, $1,500.' That or the 1968 Triumph GT 6, 'xlnt cond, tons of spare parts including 2 good engines, extra trans & too many other parts to list, priced to sell, won't last.'

"I dunno," Donahoo said, "I'd like to be more practical."

Cominsky, now he'd found a 1985 Ferrari Mondial QV Cabriolet, said, "Why?"

Donahoo thought it had been a mistake to hide out at Cominsky's place. The guy was going to be coming around. It was his place. He was going to drive him crazy. He said, he was trying to keep his temper, "Hell, if I listened to you, I'd be driving an Alfa Romeo Duetto Spider—everybody staring at me. I'd stick out like an Italian. I'm supposed to be inconspicuous."

Cominsky looked contrite. He said, "Right, Jersey."

Donahoo read the Peugeot ad again. He wondered what it was really saying. Peugeots, in France, were the usual choice for taxicabs? Or this specific Peugeot had been a French taxicab? Maybe it still was? It could have the signage, the light on top, maybe the meter? It could be a collector's dream. Cominsky would die for it. He could dump it on him later?

"Hey," Cominsky said. "A Lotus Elan."

Donahoo grabbed the *Trader* back from him. If it was French taxicab, the ad would say that, wouldn't it? He read it again. It said, French taxicab.

There was a number. The guy's name was Emil.

Donahoo called. He said, "The Peugeot? You still got it?"

Emil said, he had a French accent, "Does the cock rise at dawn?"

Donahoo said, "Uh, you're not saying it's really a French taxicab, are you?"

Emil said, *"Moi?"*

"Listen," Donahoo said for Cominsky's benefit, as though the guy might learn something, "I'm a busy man. If the car is what you say it is, everything you say it is, forget the taxicab part, meet me at Motor Vehicles, in an hour. I'll pay you full price, no obo. We do the transfer papers. I drive you home. What do you say?"

"Which DMV?"

Donahoo told him and hung up. He tried not to do it too jubilantly. He wondered if he should wear his bulletproof vest and jockstrap. He decided to hell with them. He was only going to see Clancy.

"I don't know about you, Jersey," Cominsky complained. "Here's a 1947 Triumph 1800, 'orig alum car, last rumble seat built with many modern features, seen in *Silk Stalkings,* Charger parade and many commercials.' "

Donahoo took the bus. He couldn't risk being seen with Cominsky. He wanted to conserve his dwindling supply of cash. Taxis were an outrage. There ought to be an investigation. Saperstein worried about beggars at stop signs, while the streets crawled with robbers expecting a tip after they held you up.

The Peugeot was as advertised. From the outside, anyway. No serious dents or scrapes. Never, apparently, in a major crash. The paint might have been original, it was hard to tell. Inside it was worn pretty badly. The driver's seat had practically disappeared. But that was okay. More headroom.

Emil was not what Donahoo had expected. He had sounded big on the telephone. In person he was small, a short, thin, wasted man in old clothes too large for him, a little scarecrow with a big nose.

Donahoo immediately felt sorry for him. His plan was to look at the car and say it had been misrepresented. But now he didn't know.

The Peugeot did look pretty good on the outside. And Emil looked pretty bad.

"Uh," Donahoo said. He was listening to the motor. It sounded okay. He wondered if he should look at it. "It's a runner?"

"It's been around the world ten times. The equivalent."

Donahoo thought that had to prove something. He showed his money and led the way into the DMV.

Later, headed for El Cajon Boulevard, the motor making some noises it hadn't made before, Donahoo wondered if he'd make a mistake. The first clue was when they left the DMV, and a sharp guy was waiting in a flashy new Corvette with plates reading DEALER. It turned out Emil knew the guy and didn't need a ride home. He left in the Corvette.

The badly patched holes in the Peugeot's dash, positioned so as to have perhaps once held a meter, were the second clue, and the worn floor mats in the rear (they were practically dug out) were the third. Donahoo had yet to stop and examine the roof and sides more carefully for other telltale signs. He didn't have the heart for it. What he'd do, he thought, was keep his eyes closed whenever he got out, walk away without looking, and he'd never have to know.

El Cajon Boulevard and Texas Street. Donahoo drove back and forth. He made several uncertain passes. No sign of Clancy Holden. He parked a couple of times, waited. Still no sign of her.

He thought of asking one of the other girls, but he didn't want to spook them. They knew he was a cop; they always scattered when he approached.

Finally, he'd been driving around for twenty minutes, one of the girls emerged from behind a billboard and flagged him down.

He knew her slightly. Florist Dolores. She always wore a flower. Today it was a yellow rose.

"Donahoo," she said. "What the fuck is with you? You're scaring all the johns away. Nobody's turned a trick since you got here. I've seen Greenspan wreak less havoc on the economy." She looked at him. "Who the hell do you think you're fooling? Are you Mother Teresa or Groucho Marx?"

"Uh," Donahoo said. He was embarrassed. He'd never consciously do anything to harm a working girl. When he first became a cop, the law was the law, period. No exceptions. But he had soon mellowed. Now he worried about the big stuff. Murder, mayhem, drug trafficking, bank robberies. He didn't worry about hookers, and he didn't worry about beggars at stop signs. He thought maybe there were too many laws. "I'm sorry. It was stupid of me."

"You looking for Clancy?"

He didn't answer. He didn't want to in any way suggest that Clancy was a snitch. But he also wanted to leave some doubt as to whether or not he was paying for it. Yes, he was getting it, he had to pretend that, it was the only way to protect her, but he still strove for the fiction that he was getting it for free.

"Barona," Florist Dolores whispered.

"Now?"

"Check it out." She waved him good-bye. He drove away. He could hear her yelling to someone, "All clear."

Donahoo got, uncertainly, on I-8. It wasn't like Clancy to leave The Boulevard for very long. She had her Laundry Hour, that's about all. He wondered if she might have come into some real money.

Barona was a gambling casino, bingo, poker, video slots and video poker, operated by the Barona Indians at their reservation in the San Pasqual valley, near Lakeside. It was an hour's drive, round trip. Clancy would have to spend a couple hours in the casino to make it worthwhile. She'd lose a lot of business, plus whatever she lost to the Indians.

A question nagged at him. Had Clancy cashed in early on the Willie Johnson cache? Was she blowing it under the casino's "Big Top?" Donahoo didn't think there was much chance of taking money home from Barona. In ten years it had grown from a bingo hall to the largest gaming operation in California. You didn't do that by being generous.

On the other hand, Kenny Rogers was the casino's spokesman, and Donahoo liked Kenny Rogers. He didn't think Kenny would front a casino that didn't give you a fair break. It was like Cominsky had said. Kenny would have reservations.

Donahoo thought that he was starting to hate Cominsky. The Peugeot, it was all his fault, he thought. The guy rushed him. If he had just shut up about the Triumph GT and the MG Midget. It was hard enough to think without Cominsky babbling. The guy was a menace. He was going to have to move. Cominsky had put him in this rattletrap, Donahoo thought. It was just the beginning. If he hung around it would get worse. There was no telling what might happen.

He tried to focus on Willie Johnson. An ex-Navy SEAL with a million dollars in his mattress. Shot dead with his, Donahoo's, gun.

It had a woman's touch, alright. Travata Havershot. She limped through his dreams.

chapter 31

Clancy was playing the nickel video poker. The screen showed two deuces, a six, a ten, and an ace. That was the deal. Now she had to draw. The video recommended keeping the pair.

"I think I know this man," Clancy said, smiling as Donahoo slid onto the stool next to her. "Help me here. Do I know your name? Iron Crotch, isn't it?"

"Jersey." He took the time to identify her perfume. It was Champagne. "Jersey Myers."

Her voice was a whisper. "What? You're in disguise?"

"Yes."

"Well, it isn't working, Donahooie. I recognized you halfway across the tent."

"Jersey, please. Call me Jersey."

"Gawd." She took a long look at his shoe polish dye job. "I thought Cominsky was weird. Did you wash something in, or did you wash something out?"

"In," he said indignantly.

She smiled at his vanity, patting him on the arm. She said, "There, there. I like older men." For a moment it seemed as if she might mean it. Then she turned back to her poker machine. She studied her hand. "What would you do with this mess?"

Donahoo didn't know. He had to move one of her handlebar pigtails to review it with her. The two deuces with the six, ten, and ace. If he was in a real game, yeah, he'd keep the pair, he thought. But this was playing with a machine, *against* a machine, so why take advice from the machine, for chrissakes. The machine *wanted* you to lose.

She was looking at him. Waiting.

"Uh," he said. "Sorry." He wondered if he was starting to think like Cominsky. He couldn't accept the notion of taking the machine's advice. "I have no idea. Keep the ace?"

"Throw away the pair? You're kidding?"

"It's just a nickel."

"Yeah. But I'm betting thirty-two of 'em. That's a buck sixty."

Donahoo checked the screen to confirm that. Down in the right hand corner there was a 32. "Why bet so much on a lousy hand?"

"Because you have to bet *before* you get the hand."

"Really?" Donahoo hadn't known that. "It's not the way they do it in real poker."

"No kidding," Clancy said. "But this isn't real poker. It's video poker. And if they let you bet after you got your hand, nobody would bet on a bad hand, Donahoo."

"Jersey."

"Jersey. They'd wait till they got a good hand. They'd wait all night if necessary. All the machines would be tied up, no bets being made, people just sitting, waiting for a can't-lose hand. The casino would go broke. The tribe would go bankrupt. The Indians would be back on the dole. A noble experiment in self-sufficiency would have crashed and burned just because you're an asshole."

Donahoo said, "Okay, keep the pair."

She said, "I'm gonna."

She treated him to the buffet lunch. He had some mock crab salad. She took some of everything, her plates piled high, three of them. Baron of beef, roast pork, fried chicken, mahi-mahi, shrimp scampi, spaghetti, rigatoni, mashed potatoes and steak fries, a mix of about six salads.

He said, "What's the occasion?" which was really asking if she had dipped, prematurely, into a possible Willie Johnson cache.

She replied, "Found money. A guy gave me a big tip this morning. I thought, what the heck? Why not take the day off, splurge?"

He said, he still wasn't satisfied, "What did you find out about Willie Johnson?"

She said, "There's a story. You don't wanta hear about it."

He waited. He didn't have to ask. She was going to tell him anyway. He picked at his mock crab and watched her get a foothold on her lunch. For a bitty woman, she could sure put it away, he thought. She ought to be a blimp, but she was just a tiny thing. It must be her metabolism. Or maybe, secretly, before dawn, she ran fifty miles every day. He thought that he was ready to believe that, except she didn't have a marathoner's body. She had a soft body. A little girl's.

"This is the scuttlebutt," she said. "Willie is approached . . ."

He had to interrupt. She had never used the term before. "Scuttlebutt?"

"Navy talk. Willie is an ex-SEAL, remember?" She got a chicken wing. "Are we okay, here?"

"Continue."

"I got this from one of the girls. Minnie Mouth. The one with the big ears? She got it from her boyfriend, Alonzo Roos. He's doing life in Chino. He's got bigger ears."

"This is con talk?"

"This is the walls talk. Roos hears things. Willie is approached— this is while he is still in the SEALs—by Hong Kong interests saying they could utilize his SEAL skills after he gets his discharge. Willie says he isn't planning on getting a discharge. He's in for the whole twenty. A career."

"So they arrange a discharge for him?"

She got another wing. "Yes. It's a Saturday night. Somebody slips him something. He goes ape in a bar in National City. They get him for assault, property damage, and sexual harassment."

"What kind of sexual harassment?"

"He supposedly was sitting on some guy's face. A very un-SEAL thing to do."

"It's a gay bar?"

"No. A sports bar. Straight."

"So it's not even a Navy thing to do?"

"Apparently." She got another wing. There were a lot of them. "Willie's out on his ex-Navy ass. The Hong Kong interests are back on his doorstep. They want to hire him to sink ships."

"Whose?"

"The competition's."

"So it's drugs?"

"They didn't say."

"Illegal arms?"

"They didn't say."

"Maybe counterfeit money?"

"Right. They print it in Hong Kong. They ship it here as bound books. Two bills up, three across. Six to a page. You gotta cut 'em out with scissors."

"Okay. I'm sorry. They wanted him to sink a ship. No reason offered or given. Then what?"

"The jerk sinks the wrong boat."

"The sloop? You're kidding."

"No. His first and last assignment. The jerk sinks the wrong boat."

"Come on."

"Seriously. This is the story. All he had to do was swim out there and pull a plug or something. He got turned around, off course, who knows?"

"I don't believe it."

"It could happen." There was one wing left. She took it. "You ever stand in the water in that harbor? You can hardly see your feet. It's polluted. There are signs all over. 'Don't eat the fish.'"

"I don't believe they'd give him the money before he did the job."

She looked at him. She put the wing aside. She thought for a while.

"You're right," she said finally. "They wouldn't do that. I'm sorry. I let my own work experience cloud my judgment, Jersey. In my business, I get paid, then I do the job. But . . ."

Donahoo finished it for her, ". . . ship-sinkers get paid afterwards."

They ate in silence for a while. Donahoo had to accept that the sloop was Willie Johnson's first and last assignment and that Willie had not been paid by the supposed Hong Kong interests. That meant the money in the mattress came from someone else. It meant that if Willie had another cache, there were no clues as to where it might be, or if it even existed. And by the sound of things, it didn't.

Donahoo said, "Well, I guess we're not rich, huh?"

Clancy had a mouthful of shrimp scampi. She mumbled, "It depends on your definition of rich."

He drove her back to San Diego in the Peugeot. Right away she noticed the badly patched holes in the dash.

"Hey, I think I know this car," she said. "It was owned by a little guy with a big nose. I think his name was Emil. It used to be a French taxicab, right?"

Donahoo didn't answer. He didn't have the heart. He was at another loose end and another dead-end.

"Why would you buy a cab?"

He shrugged hopelessly.

"Did you know?"

He shrugged.

"Gawd. I'd like to know the inner you."

Well, he was just going to have to expose himself, Donahoo thought. He was getting nowhere hiding out. If he was going to crack the case, he had to get out in the open, take some chances. It obviously was the only way. But first he'd better go back to Cominsky's and put on the bulletproof vest and jockstrap.

"How would you like it?" Clancy asked. She was trying to cheer him up. "I'm quoting preferred rates here. Twenty dollars for the All-American Angst, which is subbing, this week only, for the Nooner Dooner. Fifty, this is also new, running indefinitely, for the Ten Hail Marys. It may be a permanent replacement for the Fabulous Fantasy Five. We're getting a lot of positive response. A hundred for the Midnight Deluxe Special. That never changes. No substitutions, please."

"Angst?"

"You're the first to ask."

Donahoo tried to close his mind to the whole idea. He asked, "How do you cut counterfeit bills out of a book?"

She said, "Along the lines. You still wearing that iron cup, Donahooie?"

He said, "Actually, that's me."

chapter 32

Cominsky's flat. The record player scratching out *'I Wonder Who's Kissing Her Now.'* A new bottle of Old Crow at the third-of-the-way-down mark. A can of beans waiting to be dinner. Donahoo counted his money. He wondered if maybe he ought to turn fortune hunter.

He was down now to less than four hundred dollars. It wasn't going to last. Wilson Pomfret had absconded with his credit cards. The replacements he had provided were suspect. There probably was some instant track on any cash withdrawal or purchase made on them. They (he didn't know who "they" were—Pomfret, the FBI, The Mob, the SDPD's Internal Affairs, Prescott Havershot III?) would have a similar track on any withdrawal from his checking and savings accounts, if those accounts still existed. They could know about it the instant he took a dime, he thought. Today's technology. The illusion of financial privacy was just that. It was a misconception and a wrong impression. They'd know he was back in town. They'd know he was running on empty.

So how to get some money? He couldn't borrow from Cominsky. The guy didn't have any. Cominsky's eco-friendly lifestyle kept him broke. He was paying a dollar for an organic cucumber. You could get five real ones for that at the Farmers Bazaar.

Gomez, Montrose, Palmer. They were off-limits. Lewis, Saperstein. They were farther off. Friends who weren't cops? No, he couldn't go near them, couldn't endanger them. Somebody wanted him dead. They might get caught in the crossfire. Neighbors? Same story. Ex-wife, old flames? Same.

Clancy? Maybe he should have asked Clancy, he thought. She must have something socked away. But that was for her little boys. They were going to college on that. He didn't want to borrow from her—and not be around to pay it back.

Philpott? He was inner circle, sort of. He knew something of what was going on. Maybe he would pay to find out more? Hire him as a private investigator, which could be a business expense, a tax write-off? Naw, Donahoo thought. Philpott would say no. He didn't want to get that involved, remember? He's a very careful guy. He's a very patient guy. He can wait five years.

The Pelican Man? Should he track Pomfret down and get his credit cards back and insist they not be a problem or else? Was the situation that desperate? Naw, Donahoo thought again. Pomfret was for last. He'd hit him up when more of the jigsaw pieces were in place. He ought to stay clear meanwhile.

Travata? Well, hell, no, that was stupid, how was he supposed to borrow money from her? Then he thought about it some more and decided it was worth a try. Also, if Havershot wasn't home, he'd like a better look at the house, which contrasted so sharply with Haver-shot's office at the Spreckles. Maybe he'd find something of interest.

He walked over to the 7-Eleven. Made the call from the pay phone there. Travata returned the page right away.

"Where have you been?" she said, sounding needy. "Can you come over? I need a jump start."

"Your place?"

"Yeah. They're out of town. Honest. I swear to God. I just talked to them. They're in Los Angeles to see a play. They're going to stay over. Not back until tomorrow."

Donahoo imagined a few quick nightmares. Worst scenario: The play is canceled. They come home tonight. They're back in what— three hours?

"Yeah," he said. "I think I can fit it in."

"Wowser."

Jumping at the Havershot estate in Rancho Santa Fe. Donahoo thought Travata was a really nice lady. She hadn't made any rude remarks about his short gray hair and dumb mustache. She hadn't questioned his request that she claim, should anyone ask, that she hadn't seen or heard from him. She said she understood about police work. A cop, he had to do what he had to do. Donahoo also thought they were getting better at jumping. They were getting the hang of it, in the sense that they had better hang time, an admittedly brief, but nevertheless measurable, span. It was in the nanoseconds but it was there, and it was good.

Travata was aware of it too. She said, "There's that magic moment, just before we start to drop? I never thought it could get longer. But it's longer."

He said, "It is for me too."

She said, "Normally, you want the earth to move, but we want the sky to hold still."

"I guess."

Normally, Donahoo thought that he would never have set foot in the place again, but in this case, of course, he had leapt at the chance. If he could just get up the gumption, it was the perfect time and place to ask for a loan. There had to be some money lying around some- where. Maybe he could combine that with snooping around. He might find something helpful. Files, documents. Something.

He got his chance soon enough.

"You never really saw the place, did you?" she said, taking his hand, taking him on a tour. "Father likes to think he's got it all. Rancho Santa Fe and porn movies and popcorn. That's okay, I sup- pose, but if it was up to me, I'd have an observatory. I like to watch the stars."

Donahoo said, "An observatory wouldn't be much good down here."

She said, "I know, if it was up to me, I'd live on a mountaintop."

He said, "My, you're such an in-the-sky lady, you oughta be a pilot."

She said, "I am."

Right away he heard a warning bell clanging in the back of his head.

He said, "Oh, yeah, what are you qualified for?"

She was looking at him and smiling, and she said, "Would you believe choppers?"

Then she was taking him into Havershot's den to show him the pictures to prove it. She was standing beside a Hughes 300, sitting in the cockpit of a McDonnell Douglas 500D, and at the controls of a Bell Jetranger in flight, the latter shot taken from another airship.

Donahoo was impressed. He wondered why she hadn't mentioned before that she was a chopper pilot. He wondered why she had chosen to mention it now. "You still do it?"

She answered, sort of wistfully, "Not as much as I'd like to."

"Why is that?" He couldn't imagine her giving it up willingly. He wondered if there might be some medical reason. He hadn't quite put to rest the idea of her being—what was the term?—mentally challenged. "You're, uh, not restricted, are you?"

She shook her head. "No. The fleet's smaller. I can't just walk in and get a bird anymore." She located another photo for him. It showed several choppers in front of a hangar at what looked like Brown Field. The land was flat with distant low mountains. A sign said:

GOLDEN STATE HELICOPTERS
Executive Charter • Aerial Crane • Land Surveys
Offshore Work • Flight Training • Aerial Photography
Film & Video Specialist • Tyler Mounts In-House

"One of our subsidiary companies. It's had a run of bad luck. Several crashes."

Donahoo had to ask. "Any recently?"

Travata was still looking at the photograph. "Nothing I've heard about." She turned to face him. Pained expression. "I haven't been out there for a while. I, uh, lost a good friend. He was one of the pilots. He went down at sea. They never found him."

This was it, Donahoo thought. "I'm sorry. Boyfriend?"

"You could say that," she told him, taking his hand again. She tugged at him. She wanted to leave. "Tiger Barr. He was quite a guy. It only hurts for a couple years."

He made her stay. He was looking around the den, looking for something, anything, that would help him better understand Prescott Havershot III.

"Helicopters, huh? I should have guessed. The first thing you ever asked me. 'Get me up in the air.' What else is in the portfolio? Space-ships?"

"Actually we're pretty conservative. Except for a small firm, Raven Arms, doing personal defense advance weapons R&D."

"Things that go bang?"

"Yeah, and fzzzt."

Donahoo thought he shouldn't be surprised. Havershot packed a Matera, the only radical redesign of a revolver in the twentieth century. Travata's openness did make him wonder though. She seemed to be purposely laying out circumstantial evidence for him. She seemed to be saying he was a cop—asking when was he going to do what he ought to do?

He said, trying to make it casual, "He's into that kind of stuff?"

She answered, "Yes, I guess he knows some things, or the people who do know them."

Yeah, he thought. Or the people who do. He feigned interest in an antique paperweight on the desk. It looked like it might be The Little Mermaid. He was hoping to see a number on one of the several phones. There was a land line, connected to a red phone, and a cellular, one of the newer digital versions.

"He work out of here?"

"Usually in the morning. Then he likes to get away. He needs a break from mother and vice versa. So he spends the afternoon down-town."

Donahoo wondered if Philpott or Havershot had mentioned his ill-fated visit to the Spreckles. Probably not. Surely she would have com-mented on it by now? He said, "The downtown office? Is it as ritzy as this?"

"No. It's a dump."

"Really? Why?"

"I don't know. He's weird. He's had several business failures. One of them was in that location. Some real estate scheme that was sup-posed to make him his own fortune. It went belly up, and he had a long-term lease he couldn't break. So he moved in American Steel. It could be anywhere. It's mostly filing cabinets. It doesn't really do anything anymore, but it's a place for him to go."

"So that's the schedule? Here in the morning. There in the after-noon."

"There you go." She gave him another tug and grinned at him. "I understand why you may be wary of personal contact. But if you ever want to call and ask for my hand I can give you his private number."

Donahoo smiled back. He already had the number. He'd seen it on the presumptuous red phone. He had it memorized.

"You're not afraid, are you?"

Donahoo went with her. There it was again, he thought. Expres-sions of love and marriage. What Philpott thought preposterous and what he himself considered absurd. Most of the time considered ab-surd. Once in awhile he suspended disbelief. It was a weird feeling then. Marvelous and a bit scary.

He said, he had to put it to rest, "Don't you think I should ask you first?"

She said, "If you want."

He said, "Well, it seems a little early."

She told him, "It can never be too early. Only too late."

Donahoo felt awkward. Like he had just done something wrong. Like she was playing games with him. It was probably both.

He said, looking at her, "What I mean is . . . talk about different worlds?" Immediately he knew he shouldn't continue. She was looking at him oddly. It was as if nothing he could say now would be acceptable.

"Please, no *poor* jokes." She was angry. "Let me guess, as a kid, you were so poor you used your cousin for a sleigh?" She took a moment to compose herself. "But you're probably right. The mere idea drives Father out of his mind. It's why I do it."

"Do what?"

"Tell him I'm in love." The grin was back. She was going to confirm what Philpott had revealed about the estate. "If I were to marry, I get everything, all the companies, all the money, he'd be working for me, and the thought really terrifies him. So whenever I get really mad at him, that's how I punish him, tell him I'm in love."

Donahoo stared at her. He didn't know what to say. How to suggest that such loose talk might be dangerous? Two boyfriends were no longer with us. One had disappeared. The other had crashed at sea. Surely there was a conclusion to be drawn?

He thought she must have realized when it happened the second time that it was—well, maybe, like, suspicious?

"I know," she said. "Let's see a movie. He just got some new releases. *To Please Louise* and *Bone To Be Wild*. You pick." She pulled him close and kissed him. "Then we go back to bed and I get to choose."

He was driving back to Cominsky's in the Peugeot when he realized he hadn't asked her for a loan.

chapter 33

Donahoo woke up at noon, exhausted and desperate. The wrong kind of sleep. Travata flying through his dreams now. Rich bitch on a broom. She didn't care how many lovers disappeared. That wasn't her problem. She was having fun. She was making her daddy mad. She was driving him crazy.

The phone was ringing. The message machine clicked on. It was Cominsky, saying, "Sarge . . . Jersey?"

Donahoo picked up. "Yeah?"

"Bad news," Cominsky said. "Montrose is in the hospital. He was pretending to be a homeless person at a stop sign, and he got hit by a car. Luckily it was a Miata. No serious injuries, but he got banged up pretty bad. He's black and blue. We're taking up a collection to get him a present. Are you in?"

"Well, yeah, normally," Donahoo said. "But I'm not supposed to be here, so I don't rightly see how I could do that."

"It could be anonymous."

"No, I don't wanta take that chance, somebody asking questions. How is he?"

"Pissed. Lewis sent him a card, 'Roses are red, apples are too, I never saw a black so blue.' Montrose says it's racist, but Lewis says he loves him."

"They're both right. What else?"

"Wilson Pomfret," Cominsky said. "The Pelican Man. You were asking about him? He's still in town. He hasn't gone back to Washington. I dunno why. Maybe he's waiting for you to surface? That could be it."

"Maybe," Donahoo admitted. His head hurt. He had finished the Old Crow.

"The rest of the stuff, I'm drawing blanks," Cominsky continued, sounding apologetic. "Still nothing helpful on the bomb that shredded your Toronado. It was plastic, that's about all they know. No trace of a detonator. They don't know what kind of timer. It's gonna take awhile. It really blew apart."

"The chopper?"

"Zip. They've only found traces of identifying numbers and they think they're fake anyway. The ship was a Hughes 300. There are a lot of 'em around. It could have come from anywhere. Nobody's reported one missing. Locally, no one admits to one being missing."

Donahoo was still groggy. He tried to remember. "How about the local chopper firms?"

"I've made the rounds. They were very helpful. Showed me their inventory lists. All accounted for."

"The mattress money?"

"This is the latest rumor. Mob money with some sort of hex on it. If they spend it, they die. So they used it to frame you—on behalf of Mad Marvin."

"A hex?"

"It could happen."

"A *hex*?"

"A spell. A bewitchment."

"Right." Donahoo tried to think. "Who's after me? Vickers and Dugan, or Internal Affairs?"

"Both." A pause. "Everybody."

Donahoo again tried to think. "Maxwell 'Tiger' Barr."

"Not in any obits in the *Union-Trib*."

"Try a news story. He went down in a chopper. He worked for Golden State."

"Figure that. I was just there. How did you find out?"

"Police work. Can you go back? He died in a crash at sea. I need to know the circumstances, like was sabotage suspected?"

"When did this happen?"

"Two years ago at least."

"Funny. I don't recall a chopper crash then."

"Maybe it didn't happen around here."

"Then where did it happen?"

"I dunno. Somewhere in the world? Oh, and see if you can locate a small weapons firm, Raven Arms. It's not local. I'd know it, so it's outa state. See if it makes bombs. See if a guy works there, his name is Cardiff, aka Mr. Marvelous."

"Uh," Cominsky said. "What are you going to be doing?"

"Selling a car."

"The Peugeot? Why?"

"I dunno. I guess it's just not me."

"Well didn't I tell you that? What did I say? The rumble seat aluminum Triumph in the Charger parade . . . ?"

Donahoo hung up. He thought that he was going to go crazy. He had to start cracking skulls and tearing off arms. It was that time. Past that time. Them-or-me time.

Who to take apart first? He couldn't dismember Travata. It wasn't in him. How about Wilson Pomfret? It wasn't in him either. Not as much as he would like anyway. The FBI, if it wasn't pissed at him now, it would be.

He got up and showered but didn't shave. He was getting the start of a dark beard. It contrasted nicely with his shoe polish gray hair. He hadn't settled yet on a real dye job. He just rubbed in the polish after each shower. A dye job struck him as too permanent. He might be desperate but he wasn't ready for permanent. The shoe polish smelled a bit odd but that was a small price to avoid permanent. If he opted for permanent, well, that meant he had thrown in the towel, didn't it? It meant he was in a hidey hole. He didn't want that. Not yet.

He went out to his former French taxicab Peugeot. He drove downtown and found an empty commercial zone parking space across from the San Diego Federal Building at Front and Broadway. He waited a couple hours. Finally, Pomfret emerged from the parking garage, driving a new red TransAm. Donahoo followed.

Pomfret made three stops downtown. He went to Wells Fargo, probably to cash/deposit his check; it was the fifteenth, payday. He went to Billy's Pawn, where he appeared to take something out of hock. Donahoo couldn't tell what, but it wasn't very large, and it was a quick transaction. He went in and out of the semi-fleabag (day/weekly/monthly rates) Regency Plaza. He was probably staying there. He came out wearing a windbreaker, jeans, loafers. From there Pomfret drove I-5 south to Chula Vista, to a Filipino bar, Guerrero's. Donahoo waited outside for half an hour. Pomfret still hadn't come out. He apparently had settled down to some serious drinking.

It wouldn't be wise to go in after him. Guerrero's was small, and, by the sound of it, crowded. There wouldn't be much room to maneuver.

He waited another fifteen minutes and went in. It was more than crowded. It was wall to wall. People and smoke. Mostly old guys. A few old women. A couple hookers.

Pomfret was at the bar. He had a Bloody Mary. He was chatting up one of the waitresses. She was young and pretty.

"Pelican Man," Donahoo said softly. He put a heavy hand on Pomfret's left shoulder as he said it. He pushed a hard thumb into his spine. He felt him stiffen. "You've been gone awhile. That must have been a long pee."

Pomfret didn't turn around immediately. Donahoo imagined that he was composing himself. He'd be trying to get the surprise off his face. Or, Donahoo hoped, erase the fear, but it was only a slight hope. He didn't think there was much that frightened Pomfret. If you dealt with The Mob, you had to be ice, he thought. If you double-dealt, you were a glacier.

"Jersey Myers," Pomfret said. He still made no attempt to turn around. "You're a little off your turf, aren't you? The last I heard . . ."

Now there was a smile in his voice. "What's the matter? You didn't like Little Egypt?"

"Never got there. The brochures threw me off."

"Oh? That's too bad. You'd be safer there."

Maybe, Donahoo thought. But he doubted it. He figured he was a marked man wherever he went. With his left hand, he reached around, unbuttoned Pomfret's windbreaker, removed a gun from Pomfret's holster. It was his own Colt Python. It still had the pawn tag's string on it. Pomfret had taken the trouble to load it, though.

"It's very dangerous for you here," Pomfret said. "You're in a minefield."

Donahoo took his thumb off Pomfret's spine. Replaced it with the Python. An old guy on the next stool caught sight of it but decided to mind his own business. He turned back and stared straight ahead. Donahoo patted Pomfret down. There were no other weapons. No wire.

"I fear you won't last."

"You *pawned* my gun?" Donahoo said. He thought that Pomfret really was a shit. The guy, all the things he'd done, that wasn't bad enough? He had to steal his Python? He wondered if Pomfret had also stolen the Beretta. He said, "What? The FBI doesn't pay you enough?"

Pomfret finally turned around. He looked bored. He didn't look afraid, if he ever had. He looked superior. He said, "What is it you want?"

"We need to talk."

"Fine. Let's talk."

Donahoo put the Python in his pocket. He didn't need it. Physically, Pomfret was no match for him. He thought that he could snap Pomfret's pelican neck with one quick twist. It disturbed him that he wanted to do that.

"May I?" Pomfret indicated that he also would like to check for a wire. "I promise not to touch any moving parts."

Donahoo wanted Pomfret to talk freely, so he submitted to Pomfret's practiced search. It was fast and expert.

"Very good. Now, what is your problem, Sergeant? Apart from the brochures, I mean?"

Donahoo looked at him. He wondered what was ice and what was bluff. The guy really was quite a marvelous actor. He'd been a simp at the poker game. He'd been a nervous wreck in the Sand Hills. Now he was Cool Hand Luke. Would the real Pelican Man please stand up?

"Don't correct me if I'm wrong," Donahoo said. "I've got a theory, and I'm going with it. I'm on that long road, you understand? No detours, no turning back."

"Say it."

"Okay. I think, I *know,* you're a rogue cop, Pelican Man. You're working with The Mob. You're working with Mad Marvin. You set me up so his goons could kill me."

Pomfret smiled. "You know that?"

"Yes."

"Can you prove it?"

"No."

The smile again. "Then I guess we haven't anything to talk about."

"Correct. We don't." Donahoo decided to go another way. He grabbed Pomfret as he started to turn away. "What I want to say, I want to say to Molino, okay? Face to face."

Pomfret hesitated. It was for the briefest moment but the uncertainty was there. "What for?"

"I'll tell him when I see him. Fix it."

The smile appeared once more. "You really don't like Cairo?"

"Fix it," Donahoo repeated. "Get me in to see Mad Marvin. Arrange it with that wannabe mud shark of his, the Public Defender dropout, Murd?"

"Why don't you arrange it yourself?"

"No. I want you to do it. I want to know you can do it."

"And what would that prove?"

"Just do it."

Pomfret stared. No emotion showed. After awhile he shook his head.

"I'm not making any judgment here," Donahoo said. "I can see how it happened. How it started. You hid some prick in the program and a second prick came along and offered you a fortune for the new name and address of the first prick. And so you decided what was the difference. They were both pricks."

Pomfret shook his head.

"What do you want to bet, we review your thirty years of dedicated service, we find you've got a higher than normal average of Mob turncoats blown away? Is that something you'd want to bet on? Something we should check? Talk to me."

Pomfret shook his head.

"There is something else you should know," Donahoo told him. "I'm not going anywhere. I'm staying here. This is my town, and if I go down, you're coming with me. We're going down together."

Pomfret said, "Really, Sergeant?" He said, "Group sex bores me." He turned and shoved his way out of the bar.

Oh, yeah? Donahoo thought. Oh, yeah?! He thought he'd have to practice up on his tough talk. He wondered why, if Pomfret was in The Mob's pay, why he'd have to pawn the Python? Maybe The Mob was a slow pay? Maybe they didn't pay until the job was done? Maybe Pomfret had gotten a little ahead of himself buying the new TransAm. Maybe he still planned to do the job. That's why he was still in town?

Donahoo took Pomfret's stool and ordered an Old Crow. He, Donahoo, he was the job, and he ought to remember that, he thought.

The waitress was very pretty. But not as pretty as Travata.

Cominsky's place. The Eleven O'Clock News. A neurobiologist at the Neurosearch Institute in La Jolla has successfuly transferred part of a mouse's brain into a dog's brain. The dog, Rodney, still can't figure out a maze, but it can hide in a hole.

Donahoo wondered if he had heard right. Rodney liked cheese?

The telephone was ringing. He let it ring some more. He was screening.

The recorder clicked in. It was Comsinky. He said, "Raven Arms. Wilmington, Delware. Yes, it does, or did, make bombs. But not anymore. Cardiff. A mechanical engineer by that name used to work there. Several years ago. Present whereabouts unknown."

Donahoo picked up. "Bombs that could blow up a car?"

"Yes," Cominsky said. "Or disintegrate a chopper. Are you thinking what I'm thinking?"

"I hope not."

"Huh?"

"Seriously," Donahoo said, "why would the bomb be so unstable? It blows up in a chopper crash?"

"I wondered myself. Try this: It's a research/development firm. The bomb is experimental. Cardiff takes it—or the knowledge of how to make it—when he leaves the firm. It remains unstable when he attempts to use it or build it."

"We're talking two bombs he takes or makes?"

"Yes. One in the chopper. One in the Toronado. But you know what I'm thinking?"

"Don't you know the fear that strikes?"

"Yeah, well, there could be *three* bombs, okay? Or who knows how many? So why are you being so stubborn? Get out of town until this blows over."

Donahoo smiled. That would be nice, he thought. But this wasn't going to blow over. It was just going to blow up.

"Raven Arms is owned by Consolidated RKE. I'm still trying to figure who owns Consolidated."

"Prescott Havershot III."

"Oh, yeah? How did you find out?"

"Police work."

Donahoo said his thanks and hung up. Immediately the telephone rang again. He almost picked up and then let it go. He remembered he was screening. The recorder clicked in. It was Gladys Murd. She said, "Mr. Molino will see you tomorrow. Ten o'clock." She hung up.

Well, Donahoo thought. That was fast. He wondered how they had figured out where he was hiding. He wondered why they hadn't just killed him instead of having Gladys call. He thought they'd probably let him talk to Molino first. Then they'd kill him.

He went to sleep wondering about Pomfret. No, not really wondering, he was pretty sure about the guy now, almost positive. He went to sleep thinking about Rodney. Cheese, huh? You'd think they'd say what kind of cheese. He wished he knew. Go for the roquefort, Rodney.

chapter 34

The Hall of Justice. The Detention Center. Donahoo went in as Jersey Myers. He went in, and this also was a first, as a law associate, whatever that was, of Gladys Murd. The log book said she had her own firm now. Murd & Murd.

He clipped on the pass and went through the security check without setting off an alarm. He had thought, very briefly, about bringing the Python, hiding it in his shoe or something, unloading it in Mad Marvin, getting the fucking thing over with. He followed the yellow line, wishing he had a plan.

He could try to cut a deal. He could say, 'Call off the dogs. I didn't see a thing. I won't testify. You can go on home to Windansea, Marvin.' Or he could simply tell him to lay off. He could say, 'Take a chance on the judicial system, buy yourself a juror, whatever. But keep messing with me, and you won't live long enough to enjoy Death Row.' He *could* say that.

He followed the line. The building was almost new, built a few years ago, but it already smelled badly. A lot of guys did a lot of sweating here. It smelled of fear and desperate deals. It smelled of yellow remorse and mindless defiance.

Molino was waiting in a conference room, not the usual detention/interrogation room, seated at the head of a long oval table, as if this might be a board of directors meeting and he was the chairman. Gladys Murd was to his right. There was a thug on a chair in a corner. He would have come as another "associate" of Gladys's. He obviously wasn't.

"So," Molino said. He was dressed in standard Detention Center garb, an orange jumpsuit, no name, no number. No cuffs or chains. No sweat. He took a little white pill out of a brass pocket fold-up ashtray and returned it to Gladys. He put the pill in his mouth. Sipped from the glass of water at his elbow. "We meet again."

Donahoo sat down at the other end of the table. He wanted to be as far away as possible. He felt uncomfortable in Molino's presence. His madness was almost palpable. If he was too close, there would be the temptation, he thought, to reach out and touch it, squeeze it and see if it would pop like a boil.

"Gladys told me, you know, you walked out on the video deposition, so that's what's struck me there had to be something different about you, not the usual cop. That interested me. Very much, you know. So we decided you might want to talk . . ." Molino made a gesture that seemed to include others outside the room. "Let's talk."

"Let's understand each other," Gladys Murd added. Donahoo noticed that she had come up in the world since the aborted deposition. Instead of a fat print dress she was wearing a fat blue suit and fat imitation pearls. There weren't enough of them. They clutched at her fat throat. "This meeting is off the record. Whatever is said or heard . . ."

Donahoo said, "Get rid of her."

"I beg your pardon?"

"Marvin," Donahoo said. "This is between you and me. I don't have a lawyer. You don't need a lawyer. We're just going to talk, the two of us. Marine to Marine."

Gladys Murd said, "This meeting is over."

Molino said, he was smiling, "Sweetie, do me a favor, see what the warden's doing."

Donahoo glanced at the thug in the corner. "Him, too."

Molino said, "If you've got 'em, smoke 'em."

The thug got up and left. Gladys Murd stood up with her new attache. Molino took hold of her crotch. He gave it a little tug.

"Thanks for everything."

"My pleasure."

Donahoo thought that was very un-lawyerly-like. It occurred to him, he just thought of it, that Murd & Murd didn't really represent Molino. He was represented by some very high-placed, high-priced lawyer who didn't want to be associated with him publicly, so Gladys was the go-between. She was a messenger, nothing more.

He waited for the door to close. Molino was looking at him with the almost blank eyes that hid the unspeakable rage.

"Okay," Donahoo said, he'd made up his mind, he wasn't going to tell this guy anything he didn't want to hear. "This is what I'd like to make happen. Screw the FBI. We do the deal, Marvin. You and me. What I figure, I'm too young to die, okay? I get sick to the stomach thinking about it, I could throw up. All the ladies I'll never sleep with, all the booze I'll never drink, all the funny papers I'll never read. It's depressing."

"What's the deal?"

"You call your dogs off, *all* your dogs, including Pomfret, and I won't testify against you. I'll publicly recant. I'll swear I never saw anything. There'll be no case. They'll have to release you. You're free. You can go home. The only condition, it's gotta be Chicago. This is my town. I don't want you here."

"Who's Pomfret?"

"The Pelican Man."

"Who?"

"Your FBI bird."

Mad Marvin pushed up from the table. He moved down it with his odd, twisted gait, as if he was heavier on one side, he had to make allowance. His eyes still showed nothing. He stood over Donahoo.

"What?"

"If you're wearing a wire, I'll choke you with it, detective. Your eyes'll pop out." Donahoo thought this was getting out of hand, grown men going around groping each other. It was embarrassing. There ought to be some small device—like a stud finder?—that could locate a wire. Maybe he should put Cominsky on it. He stood up, taking off his jacket, which he shoved at Molino. He opened his shirt, lifted it, turned around. He pulled out his pants pockets to show they were empty. He dropped his pants and he dropped his shorts. He did a slow turn.

Molino was checking the jacket. "Jesus Christ. Okay."

Donahoo pulled up his pants. He wondered if he should say how much he didn't want Molino to touch him. He was trying to keep himself together here. He didn't want his skin to crawl. It might crawl right out of the fucking room.

Molino tossed the jacket at Donahoo. He went back to the other end of the table.

"Why do I have a problem with this?" he asked. "I get out, but you've got no guarantee, I could have you popped the day after. I could be dancing on your grave. Why would you put yourself in that position? No guarantee."

Donahoo shrugged. "If I thought there was a guarantee, I'd ask for it, okay? But I've looked for it and I can't find it. I just don't see it here. I don't know it would work. Maybe you can help me?"

Molino thought for a while. "I don't see it either."

"You appreciate the problem?" Donahoo said. "I can do the usual things—make that video deposition and put it in a vault to be played in the event of my untimely death. I could have my life insurance paid to a retired cop. He works as a hit man now. He does one or two a year, guys who deserve it. He is a man of honor. I know he would avenge me. Or, this is something else, I could keep careful watch, maybe survive your first try, and if I did, I could come after you, maybe find you, maybe blow your fucking brains out. But you see the problem, there's no guarantee? So I thought I wouldn't ask."

Molino smiled. He said, "You put it that way . . ." He leaned back, relaxed. "You've got a deal, detective. You stay away from me. I'll stay away from you. Chicago's okay. I miss it already. When is this gonna happen?"

"Tomorrow." Donahoo got out a notarized statement he had

signed. A recant saying he hadn't seen a thing. He wouldn't testify. "This is for Gladys. It's a can opener. You're out."

"Why not today?"

"Tomorrow. I need a headstart."

Molino laughed. "I understand."

Donahoo said, "What about Pomfret?"

Molino, not even thinking, said, "Don't worry about him." He said, "No hard feelings?"

"None at all," Donahoo lied.

The Kansas City BBQ. Where they filmed the grungy bar scene in *Top Gun.* Where they had been living off it ever fucking since. Donahoo had Cominsky's cellular and DA Davis's private home phone number. Donahoo kept calling and calling it, but there was no answer.

He was starting to worry. This required a certain amount of precise timing. He didn't trust Molino, and he didn't trust Gladys Murd. It would be just like Gladys to jump the gun and break the news to Davis. He wanted to be first. He wanted to get a fix on the time when, approximately, Molino was going to walk out of the Hall of Justice a free man.

They were ready to kick him out, it was closing time, when Davis finally answered, sounding drunk. Donahoo thought that was okay. He was drunk too.

He said, "DA Davis, this is Donahooie. You know me."

Davis said, "Sure, Tommy. How are things in Glocca Morra?"

Donahoo told him, "I'm sorry, but Charles Dickens was right. I'm not testifying against Mad Marvin Molino. It's not gonna happen, and that's final. How's the wife?"

Davis said, "I know. Gladys called. She was waving the sworn statement you signed. Your recant? She'd already shown it to two judges." He sounded suddenly sober. He said, "What are you telling me, Tommy? You got cold feet?"

"Yeah," Donahoo said, "and I got a chicken liver too. I'm not gonna testify. You're gonna have to let him go. It's not negotiable." He said, "When are you gonna let him go?"

"You're not gonna testify?"

"No."

"Then I guess I gotta let him go tomorrow. Murd is getting a court order anyway. It's not gonna be a problem for her. The FBI isn't gonna interfere. They'd rather have him out. They've got something they're trying to cook."

"Morning or afternoon?"

"What? You got a preference?"

"I'm gonna need a headstart."

"Not from me. He's out in the morning. First order of business. Ten o'clock."

"You're tough."

"You're lucky. Gladys, if she had her way, she'd have got him out tonight. You know she has her own firm now, Murd & Murd? I don't know who the other Murd is."

"Yeah, well, I'm glad you held off. I wouldn't want her messing around with my timing."

"What am I supposed to tell the fucking media?"

"That you're still a great guy."

Davis said, "You'll never live this down, Tommy."

Donahoo said, "Yeah, but I'll live."

Windansea Beach. Mad Marvin Molino's palatial waterfront estate at the foot of Nautilus. Looking even nicer in the moonlight than against a sun-kissed ocean.

Donahoo drifted by in the Peugeot. He wondered if there was still an FBI stakeout. Probably not, he thought. After all, Molino was in jail. He didn't get out till the morning. Still, it was a gamble.

He felt the beeper in his pocket. Felt the switch that had been turned off by Dismantler Miguel. He turned it on.

The Jehovah's Witness had been a gambler. He had gambled on a friendly reception when he went over the wall. What the world didn't need, apparently, was more gamblers, but there were a lot of them out there.

Kenny Rogers was a gambler. Clancy Holden was gambler. Donahoo liked Kenny and he sure liked Clancy. He might like her even more than Cominsky did.

Donahoo turned around at the Pump House. He drove back and parked where the Tercel had parked. He went over the wall just like the Witness.

There was a big black Lincoln Continental Town Car sitting in the driveway. The vanity license plate said HOUDINI. A nice touch for an escape artist named Mad Marvin Molino.

Donahoo wondered. He got out Cominsky's lifetime guaranteed never-fall-off stickum. Should he or shouldn't he? He said fuck it and went under the Town Car. Life's a gamble.

chapter 35

Donahoo slept in the Peugeot. He didn't dare go back to Cominsky's place. Gladys Murd had called DA Davis, and Davis had undoubtedly called Saperstein, and Saperstein had definitely called Lewis, and God knew who else knew by now. Everybody in town would know except the *Union-Tribune*. They had an early deadline. They had a problem holding for Miss America.

The first say-it-ain't-so call was from Cominsky. He knew where to call. It was his cellular.

"Gee, Sarge, I mean Jersey," he said. "Have you read the paper?"

Donahoo couldn't believe it was already in the paper. The *Union-Tribune* never had any late-breaking news. They had a problem holding for Best Picture.

"Are you sure you want to do this? Saperstein turned purple, and Lewis ate a towel. I think it's safe to say they're not taking it too well."

Donahoo looked at his watch. Not quite eight o'clock. Four hours sleep. He thought his back might be broken. He should have gotten a motel, but it was time he was up, and forty bucks for four hours—ten dollars an hour?—it just didn't seem right. It was a nap, not sleep. A guy ought to be able to nap for nothing.

"Jersey?"

"Yeah?"

"What's this mean?"

Donahoo struggled out of the Peugeot and fell to his knees.

"Hello?"

"It means . . ." Donahoo had to grab the car to stand up. ". . . that you can't look up to me anymore. I'm no longer worthy of your regard."

"Sarge. Don't say that. You don't know what you're doing. You're just temporarily insane or something. There's no history for it. You've always been a straight arrow."

"What about the two hundred bucks that was supposed to go to Clancy?"

There was a long silence.

"Cominsky," Donahoo said, he had to say it, "burn the fucking fan club membership card. Good-bye."

Gomez made the next call. He said, "Who'd'a thunk?" Right after that Palmer called, and then Montrose, all saying much the same thing.

They had figured out how to reach him. Once the word was out, he was back in town, they naturally thought of all the guys he might be hiding out with, and finally they thought of Cominsky, process of elimination, and naturally Cominsky caved. Cominsky would think he was doing the right thing giving out the number. He'd think if everybody called there was a chance of changing his, Donahoo's, mind.

Lewis called. He said, "Tommy, we've had our differences, but nothing like this. You're breaking my heart. You're stealing my spirit. I don't think I can go on."

Donahoo said, "I hear you ate a towel?"

Lewis said, "Naw. Who told you that? It was only a napkin."

Saperstein called. He said, "Okay, Mad Marvin isn't going to kill you, but I am."

Donahoo was back in the Peugeot. He drove over to the Tenth and B Street Burger King. He went in with Cominsky's cordless drill and a big steel eyebolt. He wanted to be ready to go, any moment.

He bought a couple coffees and two 99¢ Whoppers and the *Union-Tribune*. It actually was on top of things for once. There was a brief front page story, three paragraphs, a late bulletin, saying Mad Marvin Molino was being released, and that he, Donahoo, the lone witness to the Witness murder, had decided not to testify. Gladys Murd of Murd & Murd was named as the source of this exclusive information. DA Davis was quoted as declining comment but nevertheless appearing to confirm it in what might be construed as a political comment. "Donahoo has a yellow stripe as wide as the mayor's _____."

Next to it was a story about Rodney, the dog who had the brain gene transplant from the mouse. The paper had more details than the TV. The mouse's name was Harold.

Donahoo got Cominsky's cellular. He punched in Havershot's private red phone number. Havershot said, "Havershot," and Donahoo hung up, thinking that was the easy part. The guy was at work in his in-home office. He was a creature of habit. He ought to stay there all morning.

Wilson Pomfret came out of the Regency Arms at eight-twenty. It looked like he was checking out. He had a suitcase, a flight bag, and an attache. He was wearing a blue seersucker suit.

Donahoo hurried across the street and got to Pomfret just as he was closing the trunk of the TransAm. He gave him a coffee and a burger.

Pomfret said, "What's this?"

Donahoo took out the Python and put it between his eyes. He said, "A gun. Where do you think you're going in your pretty new car?"

"Uh. I thought I'd drive back to Washington. See the country? I've never gone all the way?"

"You mean on the road?"

"Yeah."

"You got a deal on the car?"

"I couldn't refuse."

Donahoo motioned with the Python. "I know the feeling."

Pomfret said, "What are you gonna do?"

Donahoo said, "Make you a track star."

* * *

The best place to do it was where the railway tracks curved after leaving Old Town and Fleet Technical Support and started a final straight run south to the Santa Fe station in downtown San Diego.

Two long blocks from Old Town, where Kurtz street dead-ended at an underpass crossing Pacific Highway to the Marine Corps Recruiting Station, there was a relatively desolate stretch of tracks, a kind of blind spot, where most of the buildings backing on the railway right-of-way were windowless. They were warehouses and storage buildings and a big paint and body shop. A guy could stand out on the tracks and nobody would see him for a while.

Donahoo figured that when a train came around the Fleet Technical Support bend and the engineer saw someone on the tracks he'd blow his whistle first, maybe a couple three times, before he decided to put on the brakes, because he would think, naturally, that the guy was going to get off the tracks. By the time he realized that the guy *couldn't* get off the tracks it was going to be too late. The train wouldn't be able to stop in time.

Donahoo took Pomfret there. He made him drive the TransAm with the Python in his ribs.

They parked in the cul-de-sac. Donahoo cuffed himself to Pomfret, and Pomfret finally sensed what Donahoo had in mind. He said, "You'll never get away with this, Sergeant."

Donahoo told him, as he got the cordless drill and the big eyebolt, "I don't want to get away with it."

Donahoo marched Pomfret up a weed-strewn patch that permitted access to the railway right-of-way. The mesh boundary fence was cut and sagging, and it was easy to slip through. There were four sets of tracks, two for AmTrak, north and south, and two for the Trolley, for its run between San Diego and Old Town.

"This is ridiculous."

Donahoo suggested they wait. He felt comfortable for the moment in the no-man's-land created by the windowless buildings backing on the right-of-way. It was unlikely anyone would spot them, and, even if someone did, time was on his, Donahoo's, side. People would think awhile before bothering to report a couple idiots on the tracks. The cops might not even investigate. The railway's problem.

"It's not going to work."

"We'll see."

They stood waiting in the morning's warm sun. Donahoo thought that he was prepared, if necessary, to risk killing Pomfret. He also knew that Pomfret didn't think so. The guy wasn't sweating.

"You're full of shit."

"Try me."

They stood waiting. A couple minutes later, on the far tracks, a northbound Trolley came at them, really hustling along, horn wailing for the next crossing, which was somewhere just around the bend.

"You think that's moving?" Donahoo said, looking at the departing cherry red cars. "You should see AmTrak come through here." He checked his watch. "Well, you will. There's one due in a couple minutes. Or maybe you won't see it come through. Maybe you'll just see it come. That's up to you."

"Don't be absurd."

Donahoo wondered when Pomfret was going to start sweating. The guy should be sweating by now, Donahoo thought. He was. The departing Trolley's horn was a wail.

"Cold-blooded murder?"

"Your call."

Donahoo yanked Pomfret to his knees. Pushed his face into the gravel between the tracks. Stuck a knee in his back to hold him still.

"You're outa your fucking mind!"

Donahoo wished he was. Maybe it would make this easier. He drilled a starter hole in the middle of a tie. He turned the eyebolt deeply into it, using the bit, stuck in the eye, to make the turns. He got the key to the cuffs, freed himself, and handcuffed Pomfret to the eyebolt. Only then did he remove his knee.

Pomfret got to his knees and tried to pull free. He tugged several times. The bolt wouldn't budge.

"Okay," Donahoo said, satisifed. "Let's talk. Here's what you've got to do."

Pomfret looked down the empty track, carefully surveying his situation. He said, "I'm an FBI agent, Donahoo. You can't do this to me."

Donahoo said, "I'm a free spirit. You can fuck a tree."

"Unlock me!"

"No."

Donahoo waited. AmTrak's morning train from Los Angeles was due anytime now. He thought maybe he could hear it in the distance. It honked for all the crossings, and there were a lot.

"Jesus Christ."

"Can't help you."

Donahoo got out Cominsky's cellular. Dialed Prescott Havershot's private red phone number. Mr. Pomfret was calling Mr. Havershot.

"Here's all you have to do," Donahoo said, waiting for Havershot to answer. "Tell him I'm back in town and that you've put another beeper in my new car. Tell him I'm a sitting duck. A big black Lincoln Town Car. Vanity plate HOUDINI."

Pomfret stared at him. He shook his head. Donahoo again wondered when Pomfret was going to start sweating.

"Hello?" Havershot said. "Hello?!"

The AmTrak train suddenly appeared down the tracks, moving very fast, horn blaring.

Donahoo handed the cellular to Pomfret. "Do it."

Pomfret threw the cellular down the siding.

Oh, fuck, Donahoo thought. He got the key to the cuffs. He was getting nervous—he hadn't thought he'd be this nervous—and he fumbled with the key. He dropped it in the gravel. He couldn't find it.

The train was coming. The horn was blaring.

"What?" Pomfret asked, staring.

Donahoo said, he was down on his knees looking, "I can't find the damn thing."

The train's brakes were screaming.

Donahoo finally found the key. The train was coming at them like a steel avalanche. Donahoo thought that he had never seen anything so big. He leaped headlong off the tracks.

The train stopped about six feet away from Pomfret.

Donahoo got up and retrieved the cellular. He went back to the tracks and unlocked Pomfret. He showed a finger to the engineer who was yelling at him from the train's cab. He put the Python at the base of Pomfret's skull and walked him stiff-legged back down the siding and through the fence and the patch of weeds. He got him settled back behind the wheel of the TransAm. He wondered if the guy was ever going to sweat. He, Donahoo, was sweating; he must have lost a couple pounds.

Pomfret said, "Now what?"

Donahoo said, "Well, I guess we'll just have to try something else." He said, "Lemme think."

"Oh, fuck," Pomfret said. He got the cellular. Punched in a number. "Hello. Mr. Havershot? Sorry. We were cut off." He was looking at Donahoo. "You read the *Union-Trib?* Donahoo isn't going to testify against Molino?" A pause. "Yeah, well here's something more interesting, the jerk came back to make the deal, he's driving around town in a big black Lincoln Town Car. Vanity plate HOUDINI." Pause. "Can we put a beeper in it? Mr. Havershot, the reason I'm calling, the beeper is already there." A pause. "Yeah, I never really liked him much myself, who needs an honest cop?"

Pomfret clicked off and tossed the cellular to Donahoo. He said, "Now what?"

Donahoo told him, "We worry about all the things that could go wrong."

chapter 36

Everybody watched it. Live on TV. There was that kind of media feeding frenzy. Mad Marvin Molino, The Mob's most ruthless hit man, set free because a cop, a yellow cop, changed his mind. It was so hot network vans drove down from LA. News choppers circled.

Donahoo watched it with Pomfret and Prescott Havershot III at Havershot's house in Rancho Santa Fe. It was easy to arrange. They'd driven over and knocked on the door. Havershot had opened it. He'd let them in. He didn't have much choice.

Havershot, looking from the Python to Pomfret, said, "What's this all about?"

Donahoo said, "Cominsky doesn't have a TV. Would you mind?"

Donahoo went around the place with them. He locked the maid in a closet. He pulled out all the telephone cords and disabled a couple cellulars. He didn't want anybody calling anybody with a change of heart. He had Cominsky's cellular in case of an emergency of his own.

Havershot remained silent throughout the whole process. He looked unhappy.

They settled down in front of a wide screen and watched Channel

8. Donahoo opened the pint of Old Crow that he'd brought along. He wondered if he should ask for a chilled glass and decided he shouldn't push his luck.

Pomfret said, "This is murder, you know?"

Donahoo said, "If you say so."

"You know it is."

"I don't know. I only suspect." Donahoo thought that he also didn't care. Molino and his thugs were all killers. They never showed their victims any mercy. They didn't deserve any. He turned to Havershot. "What do you think?" No answer. "Okay, what does Cardiff think?"

Havershot maintained his silence. It was as if he had been advised by some invisible attorney—*don't say a word.*

Suddenly here they were. Mad Marvin Molino, Gladys Murd, a couple thugs acting as bodyguards. They came out of the Hall of Justice, stopped halfway down the steps, posed for the cameras. Molino raised his arms in a victory gesture. He grinned.

The crowd of news people converged on him. He was lost in a tangle of cameras and microphones.

There were glimpses of him. He was saying all the right things. He said, "Hard feelings? No." He said, "Hey, the guy made an honest mistake, he had the guts to correct it, I wouldn't call him yellow. I'll probably have to call him in Zimbabwe, though. I hear the DA isn't too happy."

Gladys Murd, she was in there, she said, "Justice is served." She said, "Murd. M-U-R-D."

The thugs bulled a path. Molino hurried after them and when they parted he plunged into the waiting Lincoln Town Car. The thugs got in after him and pulled the door shut. The Town Car sped away. License plate HOUDINI.

Gladys Murd was left standing on the sidewalk.

Donahoo thought he knew that would happen. Well, maybe he didn't know, but he suspected it would happen. Molino didn't need Gladys anymore. Her usefulness was over, so why give her a ride?

He said, "Gladys, you're a lucky lady."

Pomfret said, "You'd have let her, wouldn't you?"

Donahoo didn't answer. He wasn't sure. If she'd gotten in the

Town Car, he could have called her on the cellular, warned her. He could have called 911. He could have done that right away, and it would have been soon enough. He probably would have done it but he wasn't one hundred percent sure about it. Something had happened to him, he thought. He used to be a hundred-percent guy. He wasn't anymore. He thought he was maybe eighty percent. Seventy-five? Yeah, that was about right, he was three-quarters of the way there, and it was going to be a fight to stay.

Pomfret said, "This is fucking cold-blooded murder."

Donahoo said, "You oughta know."

Havershot sat silently watching. He didn't say a word.

The news choppers took over. Aerial shots of the Lincoln Town Car. It got on Front Street. It got on I-5. It was headed north, probably to La Jolla, probably to Windansea. Molino had promised to go back to Chicago. But that didn't mean he had to go right away. It didn't even mean he had to go.

Pomfret said, "There's four guys in there, for chrissakes. Molino, his bodyguards. The chauffeur?"

Donahoo said, "Hey, you're the one who made the call, Pelican Man."

"They're human beings."

"They're Mob slime."

Havershot didn't say anything.

Donahoo sipped some more Old Crow. He wondered why Pomfret had no compunction about snuffing him, Donahoo, and here Pomfret was whining about Molino, who frankly wasn't as nice a person. There was no comparison.

The Town Car left I-5 for I-8. It wasn't going to La Jolla. It was going . . . where? If it stayed on, it would go to Arizona, New Mexico. It would, it could, it might, go to Chicago.

Travata limped in, pulling off a hat, tossing it. Dropping a big handbag. Her mouth fell open. She said, "Uh, hi guys." After a long silence, "Is somebody gonna tell me what's going on?"

Donahoo felt awful. He said, "I thought you were getting your hair done this morning?"

She said, "Simon cancelled. Is somebody gonna tell me what's going on?"

The I-8 traffic thinned. The Town Car was all by itself. A news chopper appeared, flying low, too low.

Travata sat down on a hassock. Her attention had switched to the TV.

Donahoo realized that Pomfret was finally sweating. He said, "Oh, I forgot, you crossed over, didn't you? That explains it."

Pomfret stared dully and said, "Yeah, it's kind of funny, it's like they're my guys."

Havershot didn't say anything.

Travata, staring at the TV, said, "What's so interesting?"

Donahoo said, he had to be up front, "The Pelican Man here— he's the guy who's sweating—half an hour ago he told your father I was driving the Town Car."

"So?"

"So why don't you ask him?"

Travata frowned. She looked at Havershot. "What?"

Havershot didn't say anything.

"Obviously," the voice-over announcer said, "Molino isn't going to La Jolla, but we can only speculate as to where he might be going instead."

Donahoo thought he knew where Molino was going, alright. He was going to hell.

"Mad Marvin?" Travata said. "He's in the car?"

The low-flying chopper dropped something. It looked like a black satchel. The Town Car disappeared in a big bright yellow ball of flame.

Donahoo turned to Havershot. If the guy was going to say anything, he was going to say it now, he thought. This was where he was going to say something.

Travata sat looking stunned.

Pomfret said, "Nice going, Sergeant."

Havershot said, "Excuse me," and got up and left the room.

"What?" Travata said. She was looking at Donahoo. "You knew he arranged for that bomb to kill you?" She said, her face contorted,

"You could have stopped him?" The question was like a scream. "You let him commit murder?"

"You mean you didn't?"

The live coverage continued. A lot of black smoke. A lot of excited commentary. Then, somewhere upstairs, in one of the bedrooms, a pistol shot.

Pomfret said, "Very nice," and Donahoo said, "It's what comes from not being a hundred percent."

"I hate you!" Travata said, sobbing. "I hate you, I hate you, I hate you."

Donahoo thought he knew that had to be the case. He just wished it had gone down differently. He wanted to hold her, and he knew she wouldn't let him. He knew she'd probably never let him touch her again. It was no doubt all over.

He wished he could be like Havershot. He wished he could not say anything. He wished he could just walk out. Never have to deal with anything again. But there was still a loose end.

chapter 37

What to do about the Pelican Man?

Saperstein raised the question at what he called an administrative hearing, held in his office, and which was probably illegal, since it had to do with his, Donahoo's, future on the SDPD. Normally there was a board that decided things like that and the subject had counsel.

In this instance, though, the only other person present was Lewis, and he wasn't offering much counsel. He was just giving his usual advice, to fish, fuck and forget it.

"Tommy," Saperstein said, "I don't know about you, but what I think, Wilson Pomfret is a loose end." He leaned back and put his thumbs in his suspenders. "I really don't take to some FBI agent pulling my tits."

Donahoo said, "Actually, they were my tits, Chief," and he said, "You think I don't know he's a loose end? We've got all these corpses but no real evidence against him. DA Davis says he can't make a case?"

Saperstein said, "Well, if they were my tits, I'd do something about it. This hearing is adjourned for a week. Perhaps the situation will have changed by then. Wouldn't you look for that, Lewis?"

"Uh," Donahoo said, "you've got a deal."

Lewis told him, "Wear the jockstrap. Remember we love you."

Dirty Dan's Pure Platinum. Donahoo was hunkered down with the regulars. He'd given Pomfret a call and now he was waiting for him. He was pretty certain he'd come. Donahoo had said it was to tie up the loose end, and Pomfret, being a neat guy, liked the idea. He probably would come.

Donahoo was sitting at a bar that went around three sides of a stage the size of a roller rink, watching a new girl named Lenore and thinking about an old girl he had only just now christened Long Ago Lenore. He was thinking that maybe Long Ago Lenore could qualify as a lost love, given a chance. He had never given Long Ago Lenore a real chance. Actually, she had never given him a real chance. But the thing was, Lenore, under better circumstances, could have been right up there with Monica and Presh and Rosie the Snake G-string, the Wham Bam Ice Trail. A close runner-up to Catalina De Lourdes Venezuela. Competition for Travata Havershot. Truly, given a chance, the ·opportunity, she could have been a contender. She was a blonde.

Wilson Pomfret came in and took the stool next to him that he'd been saving. Donahoo showed the Python waiting in his lap a split second away. He had the drop on him.

"Pelican Man," Donahoo said softly, making more room. "You're just in time. The girl's name is Lenore, and she got me thinking about a girl I once knew named Lenore." He looked for the waitress. At the same time, he patted down Pomfret, checking for a wire. He thought he just had to get Cominsky to invent something. "You're familiar with my pleasure, I think. Old Crow, chilled glass, no ice. How about a going-away drink?"

Pomfret said stiffly, "You're going somewhere?"

Donahoo, finding the waitress, waving her over, said, "No, you are."

No wire. Donahoo was happy about that. This was where he got rid of Pomfret. The guy was gone, or dead. Pomfret had that hard choice. One or the other. So it wasn't something Donahoo wanted overheard. Like a lot of other things, this was just between the two of them, private and confidential.

Lenore was squirming around in a baggy overly long pink sweater. It hung down to her knees. Over her hands.

"This was in middle school," Donahoo said. "I think I was thirteen, maybe fourteen. There was a school dance. Lenore was wearing a pretty yellow frock her mother made for her." The waitress arrived. Donahoo showed her his glass and indicated that he wanted a refill and one for Pomfret. She smiled. He smiled. No words. He'd been there a while. They were talked out.

"I filled a Crackerjack box with muddy water and poured it over her head. I was that deeply in love."

Pomfret said, "Immature for your age."

Donahoo said, "I prefer late bloomer." He nursed his drink. There'd be a wait for the new one. The waitresses were fast but the bartender was slow. "One of her friends said, 'If he really liked her, he wouldn't have done that,' and in any event she never spoke to me again."

The new Lenore squatted down in front of them, wiggled her ass. Donahoo said, "What do you think that speaks of?"

Pomfret said, "I think it speaks of character."

"You don't think it speaks of a stubborn streak?"

"No. Intuitiveness, perhaps. She realized you would remain a jerk."

"So why waste her time?"

"Precisely."

The drinks came. Pomfret paid. Lenore, the new Lenore, the dancer Lenore, started to wiggle out of her big sweater, one arm at a time, slowly. She was dancing now directly in front of them.

"If you've come to beg for mercy, you're off on the wrong foot, luv," Donahoo said. "If I was you, I'd have gone for the stubborn streak." He raised his glass. "But it's too late now."

Pomfret put his drink aside. He looked like he didn't plan on having any.

Lenore got out of one arm and then the next. She kept herself hidden inside the sweater though. It was a tube enclosing her.

"I came to make a deal with you," Pomfret said. "What I'm going to suggest is that we just forget it. We both know a lot. You know I'm a rogue cop who conspired to kill you. But you can't prove it. You think I stole your Beretta and killed Willie Johnson after putting Mob money in his mattress? You can't prove it. I know you sent Mad Marvin and his slimeballs to a deserving hell. I can't prove it. We can tear each other apart trying. Ruin both our careers. Ruin both our lives. But where's the sense of that? My word against yours. Going in circles. So why not call it a draw?"

"Even?"

Donahoo drank some of his Old Crow. He watched Lenore for a while. She had some nice moves for a new girl. It looked like she might be a natural. The tube was coming down, slowly, slowly. Her breasts emerged, popping out.

"No," he said then. "That doesn't work for me. What I want you to do, I want you to resign from the FBI, renounce your pension, and disappear from the face of the fucking earth. If you don't . . ." Donahoo turned Pomfret on his stool. Held him still, a gray man in his gray suit. Opened his jacket and took his Smith & Wesson from its holster. Said softly, "I'm going to kill you, understand? You're going to die."

Pomfret stared. He made no attempt to retrieve the gun. "You'd murder me?"

"Like you wouldn't kill me?"

"You're . . . bluffing . . ." Pomfret stammered. The beady fish eyes finally filled with fear. It had been a long time coming but it had arrived. "You'd never get away with it."

"I think I would," Donahoo gritted, still holding him. "But that's not the measure. It doesn't matter if I get caught. Just as long as you're sucking dirt." He released him and turned away in disgust. "You've spent thirty years hiding people? I've spent thirty finding them. I think I'm better than you are. If you can run, start running."

"Jesus Christ," Pomfret said. "You're serious." He tugged at Donahoo's jacket. "Look at me. What are you saying here? You want me to resign? No pension? What are you doing to me? How the fuck am I supposed to live?"

Donahoo shrugged. He didn't care. Social Security. The Post Office. Sumo wrestling. He didn't give a shit.

"What are you pulling here?"

Donahoo got a manila envelope out of his jacket and dumped the contents on the bar. Birth certificate, Social Security, driver's license, car registration. The basics. "I got this junk over at Barrio Logan. It's rough but good enough. Those guys could document a pig as a short-order cook. Your new name is Peter Zukowski. Everybody calls you Zookie. You're Polish."

"Hey. Don't fuck me this way."

"Here's the key to your new car. It's the ratshit Peugeot parked out front. It used to be a French taxicab? Here's where you sign your TransAm over to me. It's time I got back some American iron."

"Now wait a minute."

"You live in Cairo, Zookie. You love it so much you never leave. I'm paying a guy to make sure of that. It's a small town and he says it won't be any problem to keep an eye on you. If I ever hear you've left, I'm coming after you, Zookie. I'll hunt you till I find you. I swear to God. You're dead."

The fish eyes blinked off. There was no fight left in them. There was nothing. They were blank like Molino's.

Donahoo shoved a pen at him. Pomfret signed over the TransAm. Stuffed his pockets with his new ID. Picked up the key to the Peugeot.

"August is the worst month," Donahoo said. He glanced up at Lenore. She had finished her striptease while he wasn't watching. She had a marvelous body and she looked crushed at being ignored. "The humidity is a hundred percent."

Pomfret asked, "When did you first figure it out?"

Donahoo said (this was a stretch, but he wanted to make him feel bad), "Right from the start. When you left the Chevy to take a leak. An ice man like you and you got all teary? That was dumb and sloppy. Feds don't cry."

"I'm a bad actor?"

"You stink."

Pomfret walked out. Donahoo followed him as far as the door. As

Pomfret drove away in the Peugeot, Donahoo shouted to him, "They don't care at the Post Office!"

Donahoo went back to his stool. Lenore was moving around the edge of the stage. The Dirty Dan regulars were sticking folded bills under a garter decorating her see-through pantyhose. The standard offering was a buck. Donahoo tucked in a five.

chapter 38

Saturday night. The Waterfront. Donahoo was having a few drinks. Listening to all the smart talk. In limped the most beautiful woman he had ever seen in his whole life. Well, he thought. This was only fitting. This was where it all began. This was where it ought to end.

"This would be more romantic if it were by chance," Travata Havershot said. "Actually, I called ahead, made sure you were here, it's part of my nature." She was dressed in a long black trench coat. Long black boots. She looked like she might be going somewhere. She got up beside him at the bar. "This won't take long. I've got a cab waiting."

Ooooh, Donahoo thought. Ten bucks an hour. He wiggled a thick finger as a drink order. Two more. He wondered if he should remind her about the town's steep cab meter. Then he thought no. She was in the bucks now. She could buy and sell the place. The whole block, probably. The whole blessed neighborhood. He said, "Where you going?"

"Open ticket. Around the world. The first place I find I really like? That's where I'm going to stay."

"What about American Steel?"

"Philpott is handling it."

Ginny, the night manager/cook/bartender/waitress, came with the two Old Crows.

"What I wanted to tell you," Travata said, sipping hers. "I've been thinking about something you said. Remember back at the house? The Town Car disappears? I'm screaming about my father. I said, 'You let him commit murder?', and your answer was, 'You mean you didn't?' "

Donahoo nodded. He wished he hadn't been drinking. This was a sober subject.

"You were right, I did," she admitted. "In my heart, if not my mind, I thought he might be a killer, but I was in some sort of denial. I couldn't accept it, you know? He was a batty bastard but he was still my father. I couldn't accept it. I didn't know what to do."

Donahoo said, "These things . . ." He was going to say they were hard to accept. He let it go.

"It was too much of a coincidence," Travata said. "Erskine vanishes without a trace. Tiger dies on a Golden State job off Alaska?" She wiped at her eyes. "The trust stays intact?"

"I thought you wanted Erskine to disappear."

"I was just kidding."

"That's how you handled it?"

She shook her head. "No. How I handled it, I didn't have any more serious relationships, nothing that would set him off again . . ." She wiped her eyes. "If he ever was set off. I didn't have any proof. What was I supposed to do? Then . . ."

Donahoo waited.

"I came in here. I met you. It started out okay. Not serious. Then it turned out you were a cop. A hotshot."

Donahoo waited. And?

"I thought, if I pretended I was serious, this would be a good test. If, you know, he tried to get rid of you, then there would be the proof? So I thought . . ." She took a big gulp of the drink. "I thought I'd tell you things and show you things. I thought I'd put you in a box. I thought I'd make him come after you. I thought you'd see him coming and you'd never let him get away with it. I looked you up.

You're a smart, lucky cop. If he really was a killer, you'd catch him in a minute, you'd be okay, and I'd finally know."

"That's what you thought?"

"Yeah."

Donahoo looked at her. He couldn't believe it. The lady was that devious. Miss Pussy-in-the-Sky.

"I apologize. You can put me in jail if you want. But Philpott says I don't have to worry. He says he can get me out."

"Yeah, I'm sure he could," Donahoo said. "He'd probably have you plead insanity. You'd probably end up doing three to five. An agile person like you? You could do it standing on your head."

"There's no need for sarcasm." She finished her drink. "I was hoping we could be friends. I was hoping . . ." She turned to look at him. Stuck her bank robber's nose in his face. "I'll keep this simple. I'm worth, conservative estimate, fifty million. I can go anywhere and do anything. I haven't got a man. You'll do. Yes or no?"

Donahoo thought about it. He knew it would be fun and he knew it would be interesting. He wasn't sure, though, if he'd ever fall in love, and that was a problem. Most times, going in, he *knew*, there was no doubt, none at all, but this time he wasn't sure. He had some doubts. He knew that, and, after awhile, she would know that, and then the lady who had everything would have nothing, and he wouldn't have much himself.

"Uh," he said. "Here's what I think. Yes and no? I would consider it an honor, but it's a bit too soon. You've been through too much trauma. You need to get away by yourself for a while, sort things out. I also could use some time. There's no big rush between you and me. Six months from now, a year, you still feel the same way, pick up the phone and give me a call. I'll have had the time I need. That's a better way of handling it."

She said, "That's what you want?"

"It's what I need."

"Six months? That's a long time."

"Maybe. But I've spent a lifetime being wrong. This time I want to be right."

"How does it help to put distance between us? How do we get to know each other that way?"

"Distance is good. First you get to want. Then you get to know."

"That's how it works?"

"It does for me."

"Gawd."

She kissed him on the lips, a tender, lingering kiss, and then rushed out. She didn't say good-bye.

Donahoo thought about it some more. He thought she looked relieved. Maybe, maybe not. He wasn't sure. What he did think, though, in a few months, probably less, another Erskine Fotheringham was going to appear on the scene, another Tiger Barr, and if they did, he wasn't up to the competition. He was old, and he was gray. So he needed her to take her trip and scout the greener, fresher, less-gray fields. If she came back alone, he'd be waiting, he thought. She still wanted him? Held up that golden hoop? He'd probably jump.

Ginny came over with the night's last Old Crow.

"What was that crap you were handing her?" Ginny demanded. "Distance helps you know somebody? That's bullshit."

"There are two thousand years between you and Jesus," Donahoo told her. "You still know him, don't you?"

"Who the fuck told you that?"

"Father O'Malley."

He sat listening to the smart talk.

"Women, they're easy, you just gotta figure what they want—say they're big on anniversaries and special days—all you gotta do is give 'em more of the same. I never knew such peace and repose until I invented Myrtle Day."

Cominsky came in. He had a knowing look on his face. Donahoo thought that Cominsky had seen Travata leave and had somehow deduced what had transpired. Cominsky didn't always show good sense, but he did have a sixth sense.

"The night you met," Cominsky said, meaning the night that Donahoo met Travata—he got settled on a stool—"that must have been one of those flamingo nights."

Donahoo thought about it for a while. He'd have to ask, he decided. "Okay, what's a flamingo night?"

Cominsky waited for Ginny to bring him his herbal tea.

"A flamingo night," Cominsky said then, "you're standing around on one foot, red in the face, big nose sniffing the air, you don't know caviar from ratshit." He dunked his tea bag. "Finally you put your head in your armpit. You say fuck it."

Yeah, Donahoo thought. That's what it had been alright. A flamingo night. And this was going to be another.